CLOSE AND DEADLY

CHILLING MURDERS IN THE HEART OF EDINBURGH

The Black & White crime file

Crime fiction

THE COFFIN LANE MURDERS
Alanna Knight

THE FINAL ENEMY
Alanna Knight

MURDER BY APPOINTMENT
Alanna Knight

True crime

DNA AND THE HUNT FOR BRITAIN'S MOST EVIL KILLERS
Ron Mackenna

GANGLAND GLASGOW
True Crime from the Streets
Robert Jeffrey

GLASGOW'S HARD MEN
True Crime from the Files of *The Herald,*
Evening Times and *Sunday Herald*
Robert Jeffrey

SQUARE MILE OF MURDER
Jack House

CLOSE AND DEADLY

CHILLING MURDERS IN THE HEART OF EDINBURGH

ALANNA KNIGHT

BLACK & WHITE PUBLISHING

First published 2002
by Black & White Publishing Ltd
99 Giles Street, Edinburgh EH6 6BZ

ISBN 1 902927 39 7

Copyright © Alanna Knight 2002

A CIP catalogue record for this book is available from The British Library.

Photographs courtesy of Scotsman Publications and SMG Newspapers Limited

Cover design by Freight Design Consultants

Typeset by Intype London Ltd
Printed and bound by Creative Print and Design

CONTENTS

THE NEW TOWN

EAST END AND GREENSIDE

THE OLD TOWN

THE TORSO MURDER

ACKNOWLEDGEMENTS

Many miles of newsprint were involved in the compilation of this book, and I should like to put on paper my appreciation and thanks to Ann Nix and the ever helpful staff of the Edinburgh Room in Edinburgh Central Library for their patient assistance in tracking down clues and transporting weighty volumes of press cuttings.

Thanks also to Scotsman Publications Limited for permission to use material from their files and also a selection of photographs, as well as SMG Newspapers Limited for allowing us permission to reproduce photographs in this book.

A special thanks to my friend and fellow crime writer Ian Rankin, for his generous Foreword.

Last but by no means least, grateful thanks to my publisher's splendid team, Alison McBride, Penny Clarke and Susan Spalding.

There is no dedication as such, but a vote of thanks must go to the great service to crime investigation by detectives past and present, the Lothian and Borders Police and all those other nameless guardians of the law who have made a brief appearance in this chronicle of crime.

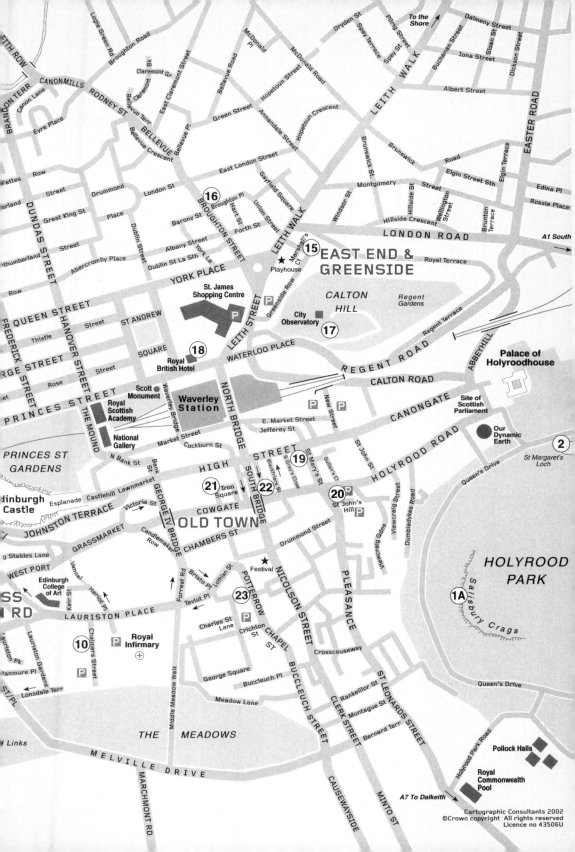

CHRONOLOGY

CHRONOLOGY

FOREWORD

by Ian Rankin

Alanna Knight could hardly be better as a chronicler of Edinburgh's dark underbelly. A long-time resident of the city, she is internationally known as both a crime novelist and a historian. She is thus able not only to detail a century of murder in exact and scrupulous detail, but can add her insights as to motive and aftermath. She has a novelist's understanding that crime springs from the society in which it occurs, and that each murder has a knock-on effect, changing the lives of everyone involved, be they neighbour, detective or offender. Edinburgh's most shadowy recesses are here brought into the light: murders for profit, for sexual gratification, and from sheer grotesque malice. Even murders we, along with a jury, can excuse and acquit. Every murder tells us something about ourselves. This helps explain our continuing fascination with the subject. But Alanna Knight's book adds to the mix an exploration of Edinburgh itself, scouring the genteel surface to show the faint bloodstains still visible beneath. Blood will out, as they say, and here's the proof.

Edinburgh, May 2002

INTRODUCTION

Beyond all tales of fiction that a crime writer might invent there are appalling stories of human cruelty, of man's inhumanity. Here are a selection from the area close to the heart of Scotland's capital.

In the last hundred years Edinburgh has had more than its share of culpable homicides – manslaughter or murder in extenuating circumstances, often with an added clause of 'Insane, detained at HM pleasure'. Fire raisers – arsonists whose enthusiasm went too far and ended as murder; paedophiles, seen by their trusting victims as 'uncles' and family friends, who abused and murdered their innocent charges; homosexuals afraid of publicity and prosecution; wives who murdered husbands – driven over the edge by long-term abuse but with no refuge to escape to; a notorious young bridegroom who murdered his teenage wife only hours after their Registry Office marriage, hoping next day to collect her insurance; thieves intent on robbery, who then brutally killed their victims.

This book focuses on the very centre of Edinburgh, but the area within an approximate one-mile radius of Princes Street that was chosen touches only the tip of the iceberg.

As a writer of fictional crime for the past fifteen years, the first thing I look for in every story is motive. What happened behind the scenes? A devotee of the Sherlock Holmes school of 'observation and deduction', I want to search deeper into the cast of characters than is possible or appropriate from the trial and news reports – particularly in those less out-spoken early years of the century where a sense of decorum left gaps to be filled in by the reader's imagination.

Our first murder took place in 1913. The Edinburgh of the day, proudly boasting of its first execution for fifteen years, was still firmly attached to the Victorian age in its ideals and conventions. Robert Louis Stevenson would have had no difficulty in recognising it, since it had changed little since his departure in the 1880s. The townscape was still dominated by Arthur's Seat and the Castle, without rivalry from the high-rise buildings of the 1960s. The ruinous tenements of the Royal Mile still had some years of life left in them. But even in 1947, over thirty years after the execution of Patrick Higgins, there is a tale that belongs to a bygone age. A young Edinburgh nurse murdered her own baby and buried its body in the garden of the nursery where she worked. It emerged that she had once been engaged to a Second World War pilot but, in a description which might have been penned by Charles Dickens, she had 'met a Cardiff man and yielded to his solicitations. Not until she was in a certain condition did she learn that he was married. The child she bore was not healthy and as it could not be adopted, she killed it.' In the early years of the century a woman who bore an illegitimate child could be consigned to an insane asylum for life. In 1947 an unmarried mother was still a social outcast, a nightmare possibility bringing visions of a midnight plunge off Waverley Bridge for any young woman.

This has not been an easy book to write, dealing with murder cases which laid bare gut-wrenching tragedies. Hence, I have deliberately not chosen the most recent murders because of sensitivity for those involved. Collating information was often unsatisfactory. There were tantalising loopholes to be filled, questions to be raised regarding victim and murderer which remain unanswered. It was not enough to pass on to the next grim tale of true life tragedy, resisting the temptation to stop and speculate when the motive was not blindingly obvious or indeed in some cases obscure, if not completely baffling.

In many of those early child murders that now familiar word 'paedophile' had not yet entered the popular vocabulary. Although the familiar term 'child abuse' has surfaced in the media in more recent times, evidence suggests its practice has been well underway ever since Man's first creation.

The war years of 1939–45 saw an unexpected increase in domestic violence in Edinburgh, where passions ran high not only against Hitler but on the home front. Marriages made in haste were repented at leisure and husbands returning home on leave found they were no longer welcomed with open arms and that their warm bed was now occupied by a rival.

Murder and violence have their peak years. Between 1958 and 1968 crimes against the person almost doubled in Edinburgh's police files. Edinburgh had nine cases of first-degree murder, for which the penalty was originally death until the sentence was reduced to life imprisonment with the abolishment of capital punishment. Culpable homicide, rape and attempted murder rose from 280 cases to close on 500, while crime against property with violence – housebreaking and robbery – rose from 4500 cases to well over 7000. Their individual histories are outwith the scope of this book but 1966 went down as one of Scotland's worst years, numbering one death by violence per week.

As well as the killers who were apprehended and paid for their crimes are those who got away with murder. According to a detective during the particularly baffling Ballantyne case in 1987, 'Someone somewhere has grave suspicions about a father, son, brother or friend and has failed to report to the police.' To that list we might also add a sister or lover.

For some it is now too late, perhaps half a century too late to come forward. Many members of the criminal fraternity carried the secret memory of bloodied hands to a more peaceful grave than their victims. Other killers, who were young and escaped the net of justice, have gone on to marry, have children of their own, take jobs, and lead uneventful lives in suburban houses. As for those more recent cases which have remained unsolved, the murderers may even – a grim thought – still be walking the streets of Edinburgh to this day. They may even number among the readers of this chronicle of crime.

HAYMARKET

9 TORPHICHEN STREET AND SALISBURY CRAGS, 1972

Map ref. 1

Thirty years ago, on the busy bus route from Haymarket station, a guest house typical of many hundreds in the city was destined to achieve notoriety as the setting where a particularly cold-blooded and vicious murder was planned.

Ernest Dumoulin, a twenty-one-year-old Dutchman, and his German fiancée, eighteen-year-old Helga Konrad, arrived in Edinburgh from Germany. Dumoulin told a fellow passenger on the plane that they were heading for Newcastle and thence to Gretna Green to be married. Meanwhile, they were looking for a place to stay.

On the afternoon of 19 September 1972, Herbert Wood, the proprietor of 9, Torphichen Street, opened his door to the young couple. They took the only accommodation he had available, a twin-bedded room. At first Wood presumed that they were married. He found they were not when Dumoulin later paid cash for three weeks' accommodation, asking him to go with them to Haymarket Registrar's Office in order to confirm that they had been staying at no. 9 for the last fifteen days – the necessary residence qualification for marriage.

Meanwhile, Dumoulin, looking for a temporary job, went with his fiancée to the Adelphi Hotel where he told the manager that

7

he spoke good English and had some experience as a waiter. The couple agreed to return the following day to live in the hotel on a week's trial as a waiter and chambermaid. When they did not turn up, the manager presumed that the low wage he offered – £9 per week – was unacceptable, as Dumoulin said he could earn £200 a week as a waiter in Germany.

On Friday, 13 October, the Woods duly witnessed the couple's marriage and afterwards went for coffee and a drink. Dumoulin had three whiskies but his new wife did not take anything alcoholic. She spoke quite good English and told Mr Wood that she did not want to go back to Germany. She was going to be her husband's secretary as he was going to open up a business in Edinburgh as a financial adviser. The Woods then treated the newly-weds to a celebratory meal in Shandwick Place and returned to their boarding house at about three in the afternoon. The Dumoulins arrived half an hour later and went up to their room.

Mr Wood heard them leave again shortly afterwards but he never saw Helga again. He was awakened in the early hours of Saturday morning to find two detectives at the door with Dumoulin. They told him that the young bride had met with a fatal accident on Salisbury Crags and they asked the Woods to report to the police station later that morning bringing Dumoulin with them. They also suggested that Wood have a talk with Dumoulin, who seemed very dazed. He had a bandage on his lower right arm and his smart suit was muddied.

Mrs Wood was considerably shaken by this tragic news and sent her husband to Dumoulin's room to see if the young man was all right. Afraid that grief might lead him to take his own life she suggested that her husband should turn off the gas.

Mr Wood found Dumoulin awake. When asked if he was feeling all right, he said yes, but never mentioned that his young wife was dead. Nor did he say a word about it in the taxi ride to the Central Police Station accompanied by the Woods, although he carried on a normal conversation, talking very fast to the two Americans who shared the taxi.

The Woods left Dumoulin at the police station and returned to Torphichen Street, where Dumoulin arrived about three hours later asking if he might use the record player. He put on 'Love Story', one of the eleven records the couple had brought with them from Germany and a favourite which Mr Wood remembered they played a lot as if it had some sentimental connection for them.

Mr Wood observed that the young man sat silently, listening. Then, switching off, he went out almost immediately. He still had not said a word about his wife's death beyond, 'Why don't people take my word for it?'

The next day, Sunday, 15 October, Dumoulin breakfasted as usual and went out about 10 a.m., returning again at 4 p.m. He did not say where he had been but on the Monday morning Mr Wood opened the door to a detective. He had come for Dumoulin.

Clearing up the young man's room, Mrs Wood found some books belonging to the couple, a letter to Dumoulin from an insurance company and a receipt, which Mr Wood decided should be handed over to the police. That receipt was Dumoulin's undoing. Investigations were revealing more sinister facts than might be implied by a fatal accident on Salisbury Crags. The couple had been walking there together a few hours after their wedding ceremony and, according to Dumoulin, Helga had accidently stumbled and fallen to her death. However, police suspicions were aroused that he had killed her in a bid to collect £412,000 insurance (more than £1 million today) on her life.

Evidence had come to hand that in Germany Dumoulin had obtained a car by false pretences and had sold it for DM5000 (£650). He had then lodged part of the money (£250) in the Bank of Nova Scotia, 136 Princes Street, asserting that he had business assets in Germany which he was waiting to cash, from which he expected to transfer funds or securities to the value of £10,000.

9

Then, on 28 September, Dumoulin induced Helga to complete four applications from Hambro Life Assurance, Brook Street, London, for insurance on her life of sums totalling £206,184 in the event of her natural death and £412,368 in the event of accidental death, using the £10,000 to his credit at the Bank of Nova Scotia to pay the insurance premium.

It was when Dumoulin went to claim this insurance immediately after Helga's death on the Saturday morning that difficulties arose. The insurance company would not pay the money because Helga had been killed on a 'mountain'. This upset him dreadfully and, in a conversation confused because of the language difficulties, it was explained to Dumoulin that, because of the clauses concerning hazardous pursuits, the company would not pay the money if she had been killed in a mountaineering accident. The insurers refused to accept Dumoulin's statement as he tried to impress upon them that stumbling and falling to her death off Salisbury Crags was just a normal accidental death.

The doctor for the insurance company was consulted. He had assured the company that the young couple were in good health and that the couple were aware that it was a condition of issuing such a policy that they did not take part in hazardous pursuits such as parachuting or mountaineering. He had also confirmed, at Dumoulin's asking, that Helga was not pregnant.

Dumoulin was very upset at the insurance company's high-handed refusal to make good the policy and pleaded with Mr Syer, the insurance agent, to talk to him as a friend, particularly as the agent had offered to help him if he had any trouble with the marriage regulations. According to Syer, Dumoulin then wanted to know if the insurance policy would be mentioned in court and made public. Told that this was so, Dumoulin again brought up the question of not claiming because Helga had been killed on a mountain. Would it still be possible just to tear up the proposal forms? – not Dumoulin's exact words but there was no doubt in Syer's mind that this was what he meant. The question about tearing up the forms had definitely been raised *after* the question about whether the claim would be made public.

Dumoulin was losing his nerve. He had never doubted that all the policies were in force and would come into effect immediately after their marriage. More evidence regarding Dumoulin's character was also now arriving from Germany.

Helga Konrad, a quiet only child of well-off parents, had attended domestic science college. For the past two years her daily routine involved feeding the cows and pigs on her parents' farm, the biggest in the village of Schwerbach in the so-called Highlands of West Germany. There she led a very sheltered rural life, chaperoned in a manner unknown and utterly alien to British teenagers of the day and more in keeping with Jane Austen's novels. With the constant watchful attendance of her father Helmut when she went to a dance or night-school class, she had few boyfriends and no opportunity for any serious relationships, her free time being spent studying typing and English to advanced level. She liked to give her pets English names: Rowdy the dachshund and Teeny the golden hamster. Even the romances which she liked to read had an English flavour, her father said. The one she was reading when she left home was about Lady Hamilton.

In spite of their apparent close family ties, neither Helmut nor his wife Selma knew where their daughter had gone when she left the farm a month before in Dumoulin's new sports car – for a fifteen-minute drive – and disappeared. According to Herr Konrad, they saw Helga for the last time on 15 September, four days before their arrival at Torphichen Street.

'We were all working on the potatoes when Dumoulin arrived in his red Fiat. Helga jumped up and asked, "May I go for a test drive?" I told her, "Only for a quarter of an hour," but she never returned.'

Later, when Herr Konrad and his wife came in from the fields, they found that Helga had packed her bags and left home. Her working clothes were discarded across the back of a chair in her bedroom, her good clothes were gone and her savings of 5000 (£65) were missing. By 10 p.m. the Konrads were alarmed and the local police were told that Helga was missing from home.

Nothing further was heard until 10 October, three days before her death. On that day – Herr Konrad's forty-ninth birthday – the eleven-year-old son of a neighbouring farmer had come across the fields to tell him that Helga had phoned to wish her father a happy birthday and to tell him she would be home on the following Sunday. She did not say where she was but the phone call, said the boy, had sounded like it came from a long way off.

But when the Sunday came, with a special welcome-home cake baked by Helga's mother, the news that arrived from Edinburgh was of Helga's death – two days before. It was only then, four weeks after his daughter had left home, that Herr Konrad discovered how she had come to know Dumoulin.

Going through papers and letters in her room he discovered an advert cut from the *Rhein-Zeitung* dated 24 June 1972: 'Young man (21) seeks for missing [sic] opportunity a nice girl with a view to marriage later.' The box number was 138 and Helga had answered. Among the letters in her desk was a reply from Dumoulin dated 30 June. Events had moved quickly after that for on 9 July Dumoulin came to the Konrad's farm for the first time. On that occasion Helga went for a drive with him and a few days later asked 'out of the blue' if she could have a friend to stay for the weekend. Her father refused. Then, on 14 July, just three weeks after Dumoulin's advert, he called on Herr Konrad again and asked for his daughter's hand in marriage.

Herr Konrad said, 'I told him he was crazy and went on feeding hay to the animals.' But ten minutes later, when he found his wife crying with Helga and Dumoulin standing close together, Herr Konrad concluded from Dumoulin's expression that he was serious when he said, 'Tomorrow we want to be engaged. Within four weeks we may be married.'

Parental consent was refused and the young couple were told to wait 'at least until Christmas'.

'I thought,' said Herr Konrad, 'that to keep the peace it was better to be quiet. I tried very hard to postpone any wedding plans until I had established that Dumoulin would be in a position to support a wife.' He added that he was chairman of the supervisory board of the local branch of his bank and that Dumoulin had asked him for a job there but had been told that this was absolutely out of the question. It was against etiquette and would not be moral to employ someone who might become his son-in-law. Dumoulin at that time worked in another bank.

And so the courtship went on. With Helga requiring to visit the doctor daily because of a leg injury received when she fell in a meadow, Dumoulin drove her there and back. Then, in order to win more time, Helga's parents sent her on a holiday for two weeks to Lake Garda in Italy. Her cousin went with her and the trip cost her father DM1000 (£130), the equivalent of ten months' pocket money for Helga. When she returned home in early September, the question of marriage was raised again.

Herr Konrad said, 'I told them that if they waited to marry until the spring I would give them DM15,000 (£2000) as starting capital. It was only an excuse to win time.'

On 15 September Helga left home with Dumoulin. Apart from the birthday message, the next communication was exactly a month later, on 15 October. This time it was that fateful phone call from Edinburgh.

'This is Ernst,' said Dumoulin and, when Herr Konrad asked where Helga was, he said, 'We are married.'

Herr Konrad then asked him to call Helga to the phone but was told, 'Helga is in heaven.'

'I just could not believe it and I asked what had happened. He said, "Helga is dead – an accident."' He did not say what sort of an accident. But Herr Konrad did at one time detect 'a sort of sigh – maybe tears – over the phone, but he is such a wonderful actor,

I cannot say. He did say one thing, that he contemplated the idea of committing suicide but he did not say how he was going to do it.'

When Dumoulin phoned again later that morning he sounded quite normal. Herr Konrad had immediately caught a plane to Scotland but still did not think that his daughter was dead.

'I just didn't trust Dumoulin. I had the feeling that he would actually use blackmail on me.' And believing that he would find Helga waiting for him in Edinburgh, instead the police were at the airport to tell him that she was dead and that Dumoulin was in police custody.

Next day he confronted Dumoulin across a table at police head-quarters and begged him, 'In view of this fact, to be honest once in your lifetime.'

When Dumoulin said it was an accident and that Helga had fallen down a mountain, her father asked, 'How on earth could that happen?' Dumoulin said that they had been married that day and in the afternoon had gone to Salisbury Crags but had returned later that evening to see the lights of the city. He had his back to Helga admiring the view when he heard a cry and saw that she had disappeared.

When the heartbroken father returned to Germany to arrange his daughter's funeral he received a letter from Dumoulin written immediately after their interview at the police station. It read:

Dear Family Konrad. This letter you will see I am sending from prison. I sit here being accused of having murdered my wife Helga. Because Helga was your only child her death must have hit you terribly, terribly hard. Up to now my life has been full of misfortune but I still intended only the best. I would now like to express my sincere sympathy to you on the tragic death of your daughter.

I must also emphasise that at all times I considered Helga my wife. Your wish never to see me again I accept. I am not a murderer.

Ernst Dumoulin, Edinburgh, 17 October 1972

14

Helga is buried only three hundred yards from her parents' home. Her grave, in sight of the house, is marked with a simple black cross that reads 'Helga Konrad – 1972'. Her gentle upbringing and background had not prepared her for the breach with her parents that developed when she met Dumoulin, a meeting that ended in death less than four months later, after a marriage of only a few hours.

Ernst Dumoulin, of Dutch parentage, was born at Minden, West Germany, and spent most of his life there. He had left home at sixteen to attend the Chamburg-Lippe business school, from which he graduated with ambitions to be a financial wizard and move in the world of big business. He then took his bank examinations in Hanover and, after a period in a bank at Bremen, moved to another bank in Hunsdum. Now aged twenty-one, on 1 May 1972 he moved on once more, this time to a bank at Bad Breisig where he was on a three-month probationary period from 13 May. But after two months they were not satisfied with his work and he left.

It was at this time he must have decided to put in the advertisement for a 'suitable marriage'. When he explored Helga Konrad's background, the sinister opportunities of a relationship with an unsophisticated girl – the only child of wealthy parents – had entered his mind. He was already embarking on a life of crime, having obtained a car by false pretences. Later he was to sell it as part of his plan to defraud the Bank of Nova Scotia in Edinburgh.

According to Dumoulin's father, a welfare worker in Meinefeld, West Germany, Ernst was the youngest of three children and had no assets beyond his salary. When he came to Edinburgh he owned only his clothing and personal items, and was overdrawn on his German account by DM2000 (£260), owing the bank DM4561 (£580) in relation to a DM5000 (£650) loan.

So what happened that fateful Friday the 13th? What is true and what is Dumoulin's fiction? In a two-week trial, the court heard that an unemployed seaman had led the police to Helga's body under Salisbury Crags. He had taken the constables to a point below the Crags after 9 p.m. but he now could not be found, despite his name and description being circulated to other forces. While walking up the Radical Road, they had seen a figure outlined against the sky above them. It had remained there for some time but had disappeared as they got close to the body. The constable said that he had shone his torch to attract this person's attention who obviously did not see or did not want to see the torch's beam.

A little earlier, at around 8.30 p.m., a young man had staggered across to a parked car near Holyrood Palace and said to the driver, 'Accident, accident. My wife has fell.' But when the motorist had offered to get an ambulance and the police, Dumoulin had said, 'No police – ambulance, ambulance.' When asked what had happened and how serious the accident was, Dumoulin had said, 'I left her for dead.'

'If he was acting he must have been very good. He was really hysterical,' the motorist told the police, adding that Dumoulin was screaming and banging on the roof and windows of the car.

About ten minutes later the police had arrived and had taken him into their car, restraining his efforts to get out as he wanted to go up the hill to the Crags.

The police surgeon reporting on the injuries which had caused Helga's death was asked if there was any evidence pointing to that other possibility: a suicidal jump. He replied that, in his experience, persons who precipitate themselves off a cliff or a high building certainly don't jump out over a rock some twenty-eight feet below the surface they are jumping from. They would change their position if the rock was visible. Without a shove or a leap, Helga would have slithered down the rock face. And if that had happened her injuries would have been very different from those sustained in her fall, adding that he would be in a better position to theorise if he had a report from a surveyor on the angle of the cliff.

A doctor who had been present at the post-mortem was lowered ninety-six feet down a rope to the spot. 'I had the benefit of standing on the edge of the Crags and looking down and I could see the place pointed out to me as the point of dentation where the body was found.' His assessment was that the injuries were consistent with a number of possibilities, but were most likely to have been caused by the head hitting grass rather than rock because there were only two relatively small cuts on the skull which had been shattered internally. Had the skull struck rock, there would have been much greater laceration.

He considered that the body struck the rock outcrop feet first and landed on the grassy bank head first. He said that as the girl left the cliff face her body travelled outwards between thirteen and fourteen feet, before striking the rock outcrop about twenty-eight feet below the top and descending in an arch like 'kind of a swallow dive'. The outcrop had acted as a springboard. Then she had bounced again in an arc before landing head first on the grassy bank.

The doctor was reasonably confident that the injuries were not caused by a simple slipping or a trip over the edge because of wet grass or poor adhesion for two reasons: the nature of the injuries; and the character of the rock face, which is funnel-shaped and extremely rugged. If she had simply slipped, he would have expected a far greater number of superficial abrasions and fractures. He maintained that the body could have got into that swallow-dive arc only by a running jump or some vigorous act such as a push.

In his plea of not guilty Dumoulin sought defence from a fellow prisoner McGregor, who was also in Saughton Prison while a Borstal report was being obtained regarding a charge of theft. The prisoner was in a cell by himself, as was Dumoulin, but they had an opportunity to talk at exercise time. Dumoulin told him that he was in 'for murdering his wife and was waiting to go up for his trial'.

17

'He said he had been married to his wife that afternoon and went up Salisbury Crags with her that same night', said McGregor. 'He was at the edge of the cliff looking down at Edinburgh, wenching with his wife. He said he got up to leave but had something wrong with his ankle and because of this his wife was quicker than he was in getting up. When he was half up, she tried to assault him and then he put up his hands to stop her and grabbed hold of her wrists and pushed her back. He said he turned away and then turned back and saw her fall and shouted her name.'

Dumoulin told him that his wife was insured for £200,000 but later said that he had insured her but wouldn't be receiving the insurance money. He gave McGregor a note and said, 'That's what happened' – Dumoulin's account of the accident which McGregor read but did not understand. There was no hint that Dumoulin expected him to be a witness or that he was to keep the letter.

During the trial a prison officer explained how prisoners were searched before being conveyed to different courts and that he had found a note belonging to McGregor. Partly written and part in diagrams, it appeared to have been written on the leaf of a book and read: 'October 13, Friday, Holyrood Park, Edinburgh at the part thereof of Salisbury Crags. The witness depends on a few minutes after 9 o'clock. He saw two young people.'

Dumoulin's intentions regarding this note were somewhat obscure and, speaking in German, he spent almost six hours in the witness box on the eighth day of his trial. Evidence was given through an interpreter and when asked if, according to him, his wife had tried to push him over the cliff, he said: 'If I am very honest, yes.' He went on to say that he had driven in a new car to Paris with Helga, where he had sold the car to buy air tickets for America. But Helga was turned back because she had no visa, and they took air tickets for London and Edinburgh. He then told of negotiations he made for insurance cover on Helga and himself and of a plan they devised to defraud the insurance companies.

Helga's parents and other relatives sat in the court throughout the trial. Her father, visibly upset, angrily stormed out when Dumoulin spoke of events on Salisbury Crags and of how he felt two hands on his shoulder blades and a short, forceful hit. 'I am sure God saved my life at that moment,' Dumoulin said.

Discussing their arrival in Edinburgh, he told how he went to the Bank of Nova Scotia and asked the manager about the possibility of borrowing £10,000. He said he wanted to buy a house and, if they would finance this, then they could have the house and his investments as security. Asked if he had investments, he replied that he had, but not at that moment.

He also told how, on their second evening in the boarding house at Torphichen Street, he and Helga had talked about the future and – as a joke – he had said they could defraud an insurance company. Helga had answered that this was a good idea. It had never been perfected but his life was to be insured, then he was to disappear so that the police would presume he was dead. He was to leave some of his personal belongings on Cramond Island and wound himself to leave traces of his blood.

'After falling down, I wanted to swim back to the mainland and disappear like that. I believed if they found some of my possessions there, Helga would go to the police and tell them I was missing and after some time the police had to presume I was dead. After this she could go to the insurance company to get the money. Then we would have met somewhere, sometime.'

Proposal forms had been filled in with Hambro Life Assurance Ltd and the forms were signed by himself and Helga. Dates for commencements of the policies, on his life and hers, were not filled in. His wife had signed her name as Helga Dumoulin, not Konrad. He had not realised that the proposals still had to be accepted by the company before they took effect, that the premium had to be paid and that the signatures had to be legally effective. 'To tell the truth I did not regard the point to be important,' he said.

19

Twice after their registry office marriage on 13 October they went walking in Queen's Park and during their second visit that evening they sat down near the cliff edge on Salisbury Crags. 'We talked about different things, things young people talk about when they are newly married,' said Dumoulin.

Then, before getting up to go back, Helga kissed him. She had never done this before, he said. Afterwards, as they began to get up, he felt his back being hit, hands in his back, most probably wanting to push him down in the direction of the cliff. God had saved his life because he had not fallen forward, he said.

'I turned my head towards Helga. She was standing behind me, and I looked at her and she looked at me. She came towards me with both of her hands. I took her at her wrists and she tried to push me towards the edge. The only chance I saw was to get myself into a better position. I pulled Helga towards the cliff. I wanted to get her back to reason, to calm her down. I pushed her away. I can't say. She stumbled, turned when she fell and went over.'

Asked if he would be willing to reconstruct the struggle, Dumoulin agreed.

The reconstruction took place in the well of the court, Dumoulin standing in front of the rail of the dock which acted as the cliff edge. The role of Helga was played by the court usher and Dumoulin stepped down from the witness box to show what happened on the cliff top. On his instructions, the macer took three steps towards Dumoulin with his hands raised. Dumoulin grabbed his wrists. There was a struggle, then Dumoulin swivelled round and pushed the macer away about two or three yards.

He agreed that Helga went over the cliff as a result of his pushing her but, when accused of murder, he shouted, 'You are a liar!' and added, 'I have to tell the prosecution that they should prefer [sic] going out telling fairy tales instead of accusing.'

He told how, after Helga fell, he had run to the Radical Road. He could see her body but could not get closer to her. As he had no medical knowledge he could not have helped her anyway.

20

There followed the episode in the car park, when he had told the motorist he did not want the police, only an ambulance. Later, the police at Central Police Station had told him she was dead.

On the Sunday, two days later, he met Mr Syer, the insurance company agent who had promised to help him with language difficulties, and told him Helga was dead. He had said, 'Can I close the insurance?' Syer had said he wanted to make it clear that there was no question of an insurance claim because there had been no cover for mountaineering in the policy. Dumoulin had obviously lost his nerve when he asked if the police had to be told of the policy.

The plan to defraud the insurance company had been thought out before he had gone to the Bank of Nova Scotia and the policies taken out would have required monthly payments of £442.

He had agreed to this without any prospect of saving this amount and only half of the first premium had been paid immediately after the initial meeting with Syer. He had arranged to pay the remainder on Monday, 16 October, although having paid half the premium, he believed the insurance was already in force for his wife.

The defence counsel told the jury of eight men and seven women that, although Dumoulin had confessed to a plan to defraud an insurance company – which might be hare-brained or inconceivable – such a plan was one thing; murder, with all its horror, was a vastly different thing and a sentence of life imprisonment on a man innocent of a charge of murdering his wife could be worse than any tale thought up by Edgar Allan Poe.

The jury were advised that they were not there to listen to a 'recital of a fictional thriller'. They were convened as judges in a court of law, and they must do so 'with all the impartiality and objectivity that is charitably ascribed to professional judges'.

'Neither sympathy nor abhorrence must affect you in your deliberations. Prejudice must not play any part. You are perfectly entitled to draw legitimate inferences from the evidence laid before you, but you are not entitled to surmise nor speculate and you cannot go beyond the evidence or seek yourselves to fill the gaps.'

The jury were to consider whether the Crown had proved three points in relation to the murder charge. These were:

1) whether Helga was killed;
2) whether it was the hand of the accused which caused her death; and
3) whether, in the circumstances of the case, the accused deliberately pushed her over the cliff, as a result of which she was killed.

There was nothing in the case to suggest suicide and a great deal to exclude it. The question of accidental death was not so clear but, looking at the accused's evidence even in the most favourable light, he seemed to agree that it was his push which caused Helga to fall to her death.

The verdict was unanimous: that Helga's husband of a few hours had taken her up to Salisbury Crags with the intention of murdering her and claiming her insurance. Dumoulin was convicted and sentenced to imprisonment for life.

At the foot of Queen's Park Drive, in the shelter of trees near the park entrance of Holyrood Palace, facing across to the stark outline of Salisbury Crags, there was a memorial seat: 'In loving memory of our daughter Helga Konrad born 16.6.54, died 13.10.72. Buried at Schwerbach, Germany, only 300 yards from her parents' home.' In recent years the seat has been moved from its original location on the now busy roadside into safer surroundings at the Bowling Green a short distance away. It is there from April to September each year and winters in the park's indoor sheds. To this day the identity and whereabouts of the seaman who showed the police Helga's body remain a mystery, as do those of the watcher above them on the Crags.

ST MARGARET'S LOCH, 1946

Map ref. 2

Arthur's Seat, Edinburgh's extinct volcano and the source of many uncanny legends through the ages, had already been in the news twenty years before Ernst Dumoulin murdered his bride on Salisbury Crags.

On 16 July 1946 Mrs Agnes Paton was found dead near the boathouse at St Margaret's Loch. Her head was resting on a red handbag and her arms were folded across her body. There were no signs of a struggle but she had been strangled. From the water beneath the duckboards a piece of a necktie was recovered.

Paton, who was twenty-seven years of age, had a bad reputation, known to the police as 'a drinking, thieving woman who had been frequently cautioned by them'. On one occasion when she was in the cells, she had put a blanket over her head and tied a bra round her neck in what appeared to be a suicide attempt. The constable then found her standing in the middle of the cells and laughing at him. She had been 'play-acting'.

At 2 a.m. on the morning of 16 July John Rutherford, a discharged soldier who had seen service in France – including the Dunkirk evacuation – Palestine, Egypt, India and Burma, walked into the charge room of Central Police Headquarters (opposite St Giles and now City Chambers offices) and asked if an ambulance could be sent to St Margaret's Loch. When asked what was wrong, he said, 'I think I have done her in.'

He later said he had strangled a girl and produced part of a necktie from his pocket. They would find the other part under the duckboards near the body. Rutherford, of slight build, showed no signs of emotion when charged.

Professor Sidney Smith, Chair of Forensic Medicine at the University of Edinburgh, was present at the post-mortem. At Rutherford's trial the following October it was suggested to Smith that the marks of strangulation might be consistent with the possibility that the woman had invited Rutherford to strangle her, and that Rutherford had wanted to humour her but had accidentally gone too far. In reply, the professor said that from a medical point of view it was immaterial what the intent was since the result was the same.

Rutherford gave evidence on his own behalf and said he was thirty-five years of age. He had been a butcher's message boy and a labourer in Edinburgh before joining the Army in 1931 and was discharged in 1945 with a very good conduct mark.

Three weeks before Paton's death, she had asked him to do something for her and later persuaded him to write down on a piece of paper that she wanted him to strangle her. Both of them then signed the paper. On the evening of 15 July they had supper and drinks together then went by taxi to Queen's Park. They sat down and talked for some time and then Paton asked him to keep his promise to strangle her. She took the tie from his neck and put it round her own neck. He gave the tie a slight pull and she told him to leave her facing the sky.

He again pulled the tie but had no intention of doing her harm. He intended only to 'humour her to see if she would not get off this wanting to be strangled'. After he realised she was dead, he went to his home in Carnegie Street, destroyed the signed paper and went to the police station.

A female turnkey (warder) at the police station confirmed that Paton, when under her charge, made several pretended attempts to commit suicide. Witnesses also spoke of the excellent character of Rutherford, who was found guilty of culpable homicide and sentenced to seven years' imprisonment. Why he destroyed the signed paper remains a mystery, but would not have affected the final verdict.

13 TORPHICHEN STREET, 1974

The Body in the Cupboard

Map ref. 1

Two years after the Salisbury Crags murder, Torphichen Street was again to hit the headlines when, two doors away, on 25 March 1974, the body of Elizabeth Croal was found in a cupboard in the Ravenswood Guest House which occupied the basement of no. 13 in the Georgian terrace.

Elizabeth Croal was twenty-four years old and had been widowed several years earlier when her husband had fallen to his death from an upstairs window in Dalkeith Road. For the three months leading up to her death she had been going around with twenty-seven-year-old Ian Knowles, described as a labourer 'of no fixed address'.

Knowles was arrested and charged with her murder after Croal's aunt, Mrs Whitney, informed the police that, shortly before she was found dead, her neice had told her that she was going to meet 'The Bam' at 3 p.m. When asked if she knew the meaning of the word 'bam', Whitney said, 'Somebody who is just a wee bit round the bend.'

Whitney said that Knowles was frequently violent and had broken her neice's jaw. On the day of the murder a schoolboy gave evidence that he saw Croal and Knowles together in the Haymarket area at about 4.30 p.m. and witnesses had come

26

forward who had seen Knowles leaving the guest house again at 4.50 p.m.

Knowles denied having murdered Croal by striking her in the face, placing a ligature around her neck and strangling her. The crime was committed, he said, by her former boyfriend, with whom she had ended a four-year relationship at the beginning of her association with Knowles. The High Court jury, however, were told that there was only one way Croal could have gained entry to the guest house where she met her death and that was with the man accused of her murder who lodged there and had a key to the room. There was also evidence that Knowles had the key to the washroom where Croal's body was concealed.

Knowles was jailed for life.

MORRISON STREET, 1960

Map ref. 3

From Torphichen Street it is only a short distance to a lane off Morrison Street near the former Regal Cinema where, on 16 November 1960, John Wilson, a fifty-five-year-old unemployed labourer, was found dead with severe facial injuries. The police made a thorough search of the narrow lane and a meticulous scrutiny of the cobbles immediately surrounding the body, and also appealed for witnesses since it was believed that there were a number of people who might have information.

No murder weapon was found. The vital last half-hour of Wilson's life remained a mystery – from 9.40 p.m., when he was seen leaving a public house on Lothian Road, until the discovery of his body.

At that hour, just a short distance away from the lane, were the bright lights and bustling crowds of Edinburgh's West End. Hundreds must have passed near the spot at the time of his murder. Yet, despite police appeals, fewer than a dozen people came forward. One description was of a man of almost Italian appearance having been observed near the scene of crime.

The police were unable to trace anyone with information about the movements of the dead man. They had shown his photograph to shopkeepers and householders in the area without any result. No relatives were traced and it was not known whether or not he was married, as he had lived in a men's hostel at Grove Street, less than a half-mile from the dimly lit lane where he was found. All that was known was that he was born and educated in Aberdeen and had been employed in several jobs, including those of ship's fireman, builder's labourer, fitter and hotel porter.

What did he do after he left the pub on Lothian Road, his last sighting that night? Who did he meet and what incident led to his murder?

Forty years later the case remains unsolved.

ORMELIE, CORSTORPHINE ROAD, 1938

Map ref. 4

Turn the calendar back seventy years to an August night in 1938 when, in Edinburgh's rapidly expanding suburbs, prospective house-owners could buy a four-apartment bungalow for a deposit of £65 and weekly payments of 22s/10d. West of Haymarket, on Corstorphine Road, a handsome house called Ormelie – now worth more than £500,000 – was the residence of Sir William Thomson. His gardener, James Kirkwood, brutally murdered a dairymaid called Jean Powell there by striking her on the head with a hammer and causing her severe internal injury with its shaft.

Sir William and his family were on holiday and the houses on either side were also closed for the holiday season. As his house was surrounded by a high stone wall, the garden was not overlooked and witnesses were unlikely.

According to Powell's brother, she had lived in an orphanage for a time after the death of their parents and went into domestic service before obtaining employment in a dairy. He saw her practically every weekend but had not seen her for about a fortnight before her death. Healthy and cheerful, as far as he was aware she led an orderly life. She had once been engaged but that was broken off. He had never heard her speak of anyone called Kirkwood.

On the night of her murder she had left the dairy for her home at 10 Roseburn Place, only a few hundred yards away. She was due to take annual holiday and, when she didn't show up on the Sunday morning, they thought she was visiting her sister in Edinburgh and had missed the last tram home.

Powell's landlady said she had resided at Roseburn Place for the past year and was a respectable girl as far as she was aware. On the day in question, 6 August, she said that Powell had had an appointment with someone at 2 p.m. at the corner of Roseburn Terrace. She had stopped work at 1 p.m. and left the house shortly before two. Her landlady had never heard her mention anybody called Kirkwood either.

At two o'clock that afternoon a waiter in a public house on Roseburn Terrace spoke to Kirkwood and sold him cigarettes. Kirkwood left with a man the waiter knew as John Fraser. The two men returned and immediately afterwards a woman came in. The waiter had never seen her previously but on Tuesday, 8 August, he identified her as Jean Powell.

Alexander Watt, an employee of the Edinburgh Corporation Cleansing Department (described in 1938 as a 'scavenger'), knew Kirkwood and occasionally stopped for a chat at the garden of Ormelie. On the Saturday in question Kirkwood told him that the occupants were away on holiday. He had a key to the house and invited Watt in.

Asked about Kirkwood's mood at the time, Watt said he was 'not very bright'. Asked if that meant Kirkwood was depressed, Watt said, 'I could not say. He is never very cheery. But he was a wee bit different then. A little duller than usual.'

On the Sunday morning Kirkwood went to the West End Police Station in Torphichen Street. Going to the counter, he said, 'I killed a woman last night in Ormelie. The body is in the ground.'

According to Sergeant Walker, the statement 'came out with a rush'. But Walker denied that Kirkwood was excited. 'He had the suspicion of a smile on his face and had walked in quite calm.'

Kirkwood's confession was swiftly followed by a detective and sergeant heading for Ormelie. The gate was locked but they scaled the wall. The front door of the house was locked but, the door of the garage being open, the detective went through to the rear of the house where he observed a slight mark on the cement path as if something had been dragged along the path. He also noticed a spade which had fairly fresh soil adhering to the uppermost part of the blade. Failing to gain access to the house, he learned that the keys were in Kirkwood's possession.

On crossing a potato patch in the garden, he noticed some of the potato shaws half-buried in the soil. He secured a spade from the tool shed and began digging round about the freshly turned soil. After more than an hour, he found a woman's stocking. Further digging revealed a leg, then a woman's body. Her head showed very extensive signs of injury. He observed that the watch on her left wrist had stopped at 5.22.

By the time the woman's naked body had been removed, the keys to the house produced by Kirkwood revealed very extensive bloodstains stretching from the back door to the staircase. Linoleum, which covered the passageway, was also badly stained.

Upstairs the detective saw a pail containing a brownish coloured liquid and also a scrubbing brush. There was a hammer as well, badly bloodstained all over and with several hairs stuck beneath the splintered wood near the head, and a bundle in the corridor wrapped in the cover removed from the sofa in the music room. This contained a lady's coat, other articles of clothing and two cushions. The cover was bloodstained where a portion of the cushion had touched it. In the music room someone had obviously made an attempt to clean up and the carpet had been shifted to the side. On a nest of tables were a bottle of sherry, three tumblers – two intact and one broken – an ashtray with cigarette butts, a foreign coin – a franc – a box of matches and some broken glass.

Evidence that 'tremendous violence' had been used was given by the principal police surgeon who had been at the garden when the body was disinterred. The woman had met her death at approximately 4 p.m. on the Saturday afternoon. Death was due to shock and a shattered skull, while bruises on her neck suggested she had been seized by the throat. The blows indicated that Powell had been lying on the sofa moving her head in an effort to dodge the blows. Stains on Kirkwood's shirt were caused by spurts of blood.

Kirkwood's father said that his son had been subject to epileptic fits in his youth, and Kirkwood showed signs of emotion while he was in the witness box, at intervals wiping away tears during the questioning. He was born in September 1907 and had suffered from infantile paralysis at the age of four. When he was in his late teens he had begun to take fits and was subject to attacks for three or four years, sometimes taking three or four in one day with a few days' interval before the fits came on again. According to his father, at such times he sometimes fell down and collapsed altogether and at others he became violent and developed great strength. On one occasion after the family moved to Dunfermline, Kirkwood left home saying he was going to join a ship and was found in a fit lying on the road. He responded to treatment at Glasgow Royal Infirmary for this condition and the last time his father knew of him taking a fit was about ten years earlier, in 1928.

When the family went to live at Upper Largo, Kirkwood's mother found that he had some arsenic in his possession. His parents were alarmed, although Kirkwood insisted it was for killing weeds or something in some woman's garden. Failing to persuade him to give it up, his father notified the police, who found it in the bank of a nearby burn.

Visiting his parents, Kirkwood's behaviour was often odd. He would ask his mother for aspirins and, although there were no warning signs beforehand, he would stop in the middle of a conversation and look as if he were thinking, carrying on the conversation exactly where he had stopped a little while later. He was once found wandering in Port Glasgow by a policeman and did not know where he was or how he had got there.

A professor from the Hospital for Mental Disorders in Glasgow said that he recognised Kirkwood, having seen him some two and a half years earlier at the Royal Infirmary when he was suffering from arsenic poisoning in what amounted to an attempted suicide. The court was also told that he had once swallowed poison after a quarrel with his wife. However, there were no indications of hallucinations or delusions, and his memory and intellectual faculties seemed well preserved. The conclusion was that Kirkwood was sane, despite his earlier medical record of infantile paralysis and epilepsy, and that, at the time of the murder of Powell, he knew what he was doing but as an epileptic did not have the same restraint as would control a normal or sane person. He was not a fully responsible individual and the crime was committed under the influence of an epileptic seizure. Kirkwood pleaded guilty as charged.

In passing sentence the judge said, 'You have pleaded guilty to a most appalling crime. You inflicted terrible injuries upon this woman. You took her life and afterwards you buried her body in the garden. The only sentence I can pronounce upon you that can be in any way commensurate with the crime you have committed and be adequate in the public interest is that you be detained in penal servitude for life.' Kirkwood listened to the verdict apparently unmoved.

Was Powell as respectable as everyone made out? Or had the excitement of an illicit rendezvous in the posh house gone too far and ended in tragedy? We'll never know. Nor will we find out why Kirkwood invited Watt in to see the house, or whether Powell was already lying dead upstairs in the music room while Watt became an unwitting alibi for the murderer.

DALRY AND FOUNTAINBRIDGE

31 SLATEFORD ROAD, 1973

The Betting Shop Murder

Map ref. 5

Like the Torso Murder which concludes this chronicle of Edinburgh's killers (*see* p.145) Slateford Road is strictly speaking outwith the 'murder mile' radius of this book. Both cases are included as examples of the exceptional skills and perseverance of the Edinburgh City Police in tracking down the killers involved.

A short walk south from Corstorphine Road brings you to Slateford Road where a betting shop murder brought with it all the ingredients of a *Taggart* drama. Here are cops and robbers on the job, tracking down a killer and leaving literally no stone unturned, their painstaking investigations at last rewarded – because of a betting slip left by the murderer.

This is the way it happened. Douglas Rhodes Knowles set out on the evening of 28 February with the intention of robbing his local bookie's shop at no. 91 Slateford Road. Why else should he take a claw hammer? He obviously considered the possibility of fingerprints too because he wrapped two handkerchiefs round the shaft and head. While he stood cold-bloodedly contemplating his next move in the shop, he watched Alex Stewart, the betting shop owner, prepare three betting slips, which Knowles was careful not to sign with either his name or nom de plume before striking Stewart a death blow with the hammer.

When he calmly walked out of the shop with the £568 he had stolen, he believed he had got away with murder. However, Knowles did not reckon on the perseverance of the Lothian and Borders Police forensics squad. It is now a well-known and accepted fact both to detectives and crime fiction writers that it is well nigh impossible for someone to commit a crime without either leaving something at the scene or taking away something from it. DI John Veitch was one of the first branch officers to get to the murder scene, accompanied by the usual Scene of Crime (SOC) squad of four detectives, bringing with them the 'murder bag' containing everything needed for gathering clues and hoping as always to find the area around the body and the contents of the premises undisturbed – exactly as they were when the killer made his getaway.

DI Veitch was seeking two things: what the murderer had brought into the betting shop with him and left there; and what evidence he had taken away with him.

Today the advent of genetic fingerprinting and the progress of forensic science present a very different scene from the crime procedure of two policemen back in 1926 who, after the murder of Bertha Merrett by her son Donald, calmly proceeded to 'tidy up' therefore removing any possible fingerprints or clues (*see* p. 71)!

'A murder inside a building is usually easier to solve than one that takes place outside,' said DI Veitch. 'There is usually a link with the building, the victim and the murderer. Most knowledge gained stems from among the victim's associates.'

The betting shop wasn't short of possible clues. It yielded fingerprints, footprints, blood samples and the usual scene-of-crime debris that, square yard by square yard, is methodically taken by the police, placed in polythene bags and labelled. Among the litter, of course, were many discarded, crumpled-up betting slips. And one in the basket on the office side of the counter. But there was no obvious murder weapon lying around.

Some kind of blunt instrument, the pathologist told them, was what they were on the lookout for.

It turned up two days later half a mile away. A claw hammer, wrapped in blood-clotted handkerchiefs and a roller towel, hanging from barbed wire on top of a wall in Robertson Avenue. There were no fingerprints to be got from the carefully wrapped hammer shaft, of course. But the handkerchiefs themselves yielded valuable clues: two ordinary white handkerchiefs, except that one had the letter 'L' embroidered in blue on one corner and the other the initial 'D'. Tracing the origins of those handkerchiefs became a priority, especially the one with initial 'L', as DI Veitch didn't think there would be as many men's names beginning with that letter as other initials.

Meanwhile, DCI Norman Deland, head of the scientific branch, was embarking on an astonishing line of enquiry in another direction. He had learned that Stewart's wife had phoned him at 5.40 p.m. that evening and had arranged to pick him up at the betting shop at 6 p.m.

Between these two times, witnesses living above the betting shop had heard screaming from below. They recalled that a particular item of news about Vietnam was being screened on television. From a timed script made available by the BBC, they discovered that the item had been run between 5.53 and 5.54 p.m., so the exact timing of the murder was established beyond doubt.

The BBC script was one of the biggest breaks the detectives had on the case. As it turned out, the single betting slip with serial number 5536 found in the basket behind the counter had been passed through the official time-stamping clock at 17.31 – or 5.31 p.m. The bet bearing the previous number – 5535 – had been dealt with and cleared prior to 5 p.m.

The handwriting on betting slip 5536 related to a football match being played in Edinburgh that evening, and was in the following terms: '£1 Win. Hibs. 6/4 to Win'. It bore no name, but on the floor, among many spoiled slips and other papers, were two other betting slips, each bearing a partly completed handwritten bet: '£1 Win'. These two slips had not been time-stamped and again bore no nom de plume.

To DCI Deland the time of the screams and the time on betting slip 5536 were so close that it was at least a possibility that who-ever had written that slip could be Stewart's murderer. After careful comparison of the writing on the two discarded slips and the one found in the basket, it was also agreed by the investigat-ing team that there was 'a strong degree of probability' that all three were written by the same person.

This information set in motion one of the most laborious searches police officers were ever obliged to make. Every betting slip that had passed through the office that day was noted and, in addition, those dating right back to the previous December were examined. The results were disappointing. Not one threw up a slip with the same distinctive writing and the detectives still had no clue to the murderer's identity. There remained only the faint hope that following through the betting slip inquiry might still reveal it.

A decision was made to extend the search. The nearest rival bet-ting office to that of the scene of the crime was chosen – Dan Flynn's, about a hundred yards away. And there, every betting slip from the beginning of February to the day of the murder was examined but again with a disappointing lack of success.

The search doggedly continued and, on 9 March, nine days after the murder, a number of betting slips containing all the writ-ing characteristics they were looking for turned up. Many bore nom de plumes – 'DK', 'Betty 328' and 'D. Knowles'. And the bets were numerous enough to hint that the author was some kind of compulsive gambler. One slip in particular, a football bet signed 'DK', was dated the day of the murder.

Then the detectives had a stroke of luck. The betting office staff at Flynn's offered a suggestion as to the identity of 'D. Knowles', who was traced and brought to police headquarters. Was this the betting shop murderer, a man who had left something incriminating at the scene of his crime?

Knowles was shown four slips from Flynn's office and admitted writing them . . . But he denied, after some hesitation, having been to the other betting office in Slateford Road on the murder date. Asked if he would be willing to supply samples of his handwriting, he readily agreed. To dictation he wrote on the face of thirteen blank betting slips the exact words and figures appearing on the three murder-scene slips. None seemed to correspond.

Knowles was then asked to write on the reverse side of two of the specimen forms. The words '£1 Win' were chosen, to be written several times and quickly. Knowles did as asked, and unwittingly provided on the second of these forms five perfect examples of exactly what the detectives were looking for. But although DCI Deland was now certain that Knowles was the man who had written the three betting slips and murdered Stewart, it was decided he should be released until they had followed up Knowles' betting activities *after* the murder.

Even judged against murder-hunt standards, the task the police undertook was daunting. Almost 25,000 betting slips from seven other Edinburgh betting shops were examined. From the massive search, 384 written by Knowles were found. These represented overall stakes of £538 for a return of £642 during the nine-day period after Stewart's body was found and this information convinced the scientific branch that their exhaustive inquiries linked Knowles with the murder scene. On 6 April he was arrested on a charge of murder and theft by housebreaking.

Meanwhile, DI Veitch had been pursuing an inquiry regarding the origin and ownership of the two initialled handkerchiefs the killer had wrapped around the handle of the murder weapon. And by an amazing coincidence when Knowles was arrested he was found to have a similar handkerchief on him, with the initial 'L' embroidered in blue thread in one corner.

Immediate inquiries around retailers and wholesalers in

Edinburgh's drapery trade led further afield, down to the cotton manufacturing area of Lancashire. A lead in Manchester took them to the laboratory of Marks and Spencer in London. It confirmed that the handkerchiefs had at one time been sold by them and that they were obtained from Northern Ireland. So off the detectives went, over the Irish Sea to factories that made handkerchiefs and businesses that did embroidery in Belfast, Lurgan, Portadown and Lisburn.

'We ended up following leads that took us down little farm tracks to folk who did embroidery in little sheds at the bottom of their gardens. Then we had a piece of luck,' said DI Veitch. 'The production manager of a factory in Portadown, who had once been in the embroidery business, recognised the "L" on the handkerchief as an initial he had embroidered himself – one of a set of only 144!'

It was then discovered that Knowles had been given a box of handkerchiefs along with other possessions from a dead aunt who had bought them for his uncle. And the handkerchiefs which Knowles had used around the claw hammer proved to be two of a set of three. Further evidence by the scientific branch also revealed a red mark on the murder handkerchief, which was shown by chromatography to have been caused by a red Biro. Similar stains were found inside Knowles' jacket pocket.

Knowles had left the unlikeliest clue – his own handwriting – at the murder scene and had brought two initialled handkerchiefs to the betting shop and away from it afterwards. That the hammer and handkerchiefs were linked with the murder was in no further doubt since Knowles had wrapped his bloodstained weapon in a roller towel . . . from the murder shop toilet!

He was jailed for life.

DALRY CEMETERY, 1976

Map ref. 6

From Slateford Road, return towards the city centre. Go to Dalry Cemetery where, on a bitter winter day on 23 January 1976, a woman was walking her Labrador who sniffed out the body of a man lying near a derelict crypt. It was known locally as a 'haunt for hippies', strewn with empty cans and bottles and disposable syringes.

The dead man, who had a knife clasped in his hand, was Charles McPhail, former son-in-law of the retired chief constable, Sir John Inch. McPhail's grandfather was a former editor of the *Edinburgh Evening News* and Charles had inherited more than £20,000 from his estate. He had worked as a press photographer with the *Evening Dispatch* and had married Ann Inch in 1969. Their marriage had ended in 1972 when McPhail, serving a sentence in Peterhead prison, sued for divorce. The tragic story of a man who had opted out of a promising life, ended with a last known address in a city lodging-house where he was staying at the time of his death.

The police did not have far to search for his killer among the hippies and drug addicts who were his acquaintances at the Dalry Cemetery crypt. McPhail and George Stevenson had been at loggerheads. There were whispers and hints of violence, and Stevenson was arrested around Valentine's Day, accused of McPhail's murder. He had been fighting with McPhail and was observed throwing him to the ground, punching and striking him on the face and head with a stone or similar object. Stevenson lodged a special plea of self-defence, however, claiming that McPhail had assaulted him first. Noisy scenes of violence between the two men, high on drugs and wine, were commonplace.

Among those giving evidence was a young woman, Morag Smith, who said that she and Stevenson shared a flat in Yeaman Place and were involved in a 'scene where people take themselves out of this world for a "wee while" either through drink or drugs'. She did not know if McPhail took drugs but agreed that he was a heavy drinker.

Stevenson, described as an alcoholic, admitted to thirty-four previous convictions. His plea of self-defence – based on the evidence of McPhail being found with a knife in his hand – got him a prison sentence of seven years.

YEAMAN PLACE, 1987

Map ref. 7

Across the Western Approach Road on to Dundee Street leads to Yeaman Place where twenty-year-old Ann Ballantyne went missing from her home in November 1987.

She was last seen alive by her mother as she left the family home in Warriston Road to return to her flat where she lived alone. Five days later a friend alerted the family that Ann had failed to turn up for an arranged meeting.

Her mother thought she had perhaps needed some time out on her own and visited Ann's flat leaving notes for her. She had a good relationship with her family – a pretty girl, unemployed but confident of finding a job soon.

She loved music, heavy metal and clubbing and went often to the Venue in Calton Road. Her wide circle of friends – as well as classmates from her old school Trinity Academy – included members of the 'biker fraternity'.

When she failed to turn up on Christmas Eve, her mother was truly alarmed. Her daughter would never have missed Christmas at home, a big family occasion that she loved. Next day Mrs Ballantyne went to the police station. The police immediately conducted extensive door-to-door inquiries and questioned her friends and ex-fiancé Joe Burden, who at that time lived in a flat in Grove Street. They had recently split up but remained good friends.

A massive search operation was carried out and an incident room set up, but Ann's whereabouts remained a complete mystery until two months later. On 21 January 1988 her stepfather Graham came home after visiting a garage near the canal by Ann's flat to tell his wife that the body of a woman had been found.

Three men walking near the canal had found Ann's body under Walker Bridge less than a hundred yards from her home, wrapped in a cloth bundle close to the busy towpath. Police tests revealed that it had only lain in the water for a few days but there were no means of finding the exact time of death. The surface of the water, frozen for several days, had partially thawed.

Two months is a long time for police to track back for murder clues and, fourteen years later, mystery still surrounds her death. In the time that has elapsed since Ann's disappearance, there has been no arrest, no fatal accident inquiry and no public statement which would shed light on the case. Although the family had given the police certain information, they were under orders for secrecy from the Procurator Fiscal's office. According to Ann's stepfather, they had been told not to give out any details; that everything was supposed to be confidential because there had not yet been a trial. He hoped that there would be one 'at the end of the day and that someone will be brought to justice. All we can do is wait and wonder.'

That statement was made at the time of the discovery of Ann's body. He later added that, 'Whoever is responsible has been very clever and has hidden his tracks well. Unless someone breaks or talks, I can't see the authorities getting someone for it.' The grim discovery had sparked off an intensive murder inquiry which lasted for several months, but the riddle of Ann's final hours has never been fully solved.

At the start of the inquiry, the police said their information suggested that the body might have been wrapped in cloth material 'in some manner', refusing to comment on whether or not it had been tied up. They only ever referred to the death as 'suspicious' but consistently refused to reveal the cause of death. According to the death certificate, issued after the post-mortem, Ann had died from the combined effects of 'asphyxia and vagal inhibition' (the heart stopped beating) and a 'ligature around the neck'.

An attempt was made to progress the case using genetic finger-printing and samples were sent to England for DNA profiling. However, it proved impossible to draw any conclusions because the body had been in the water too long. All the police forensic squads had to go on was the hope that a witness might come forward who had seen what appeared to be a bundle being carried or dumped in the water in the area.

The police had one suspect but no charges were ever brought against him. They now believe that her killer kept her body hidden until it was dumped in the canal, but where she was kept before that remains a mystery.

No one can say for sure what happened to Ann in the weeks between her disappearance and the discovery of her body. Police frogmen searched the rubbish-strewn canal for clues. Her black shoulder bag, black leather jerkin, a brass petrol lighter with her initials and two keys on a keyring were never recovered. A camera and a small brown photo album were also missing from her home.

Ann Ballantyne's murder remains unsolved.

Had there been any evidence of forced entry into Ann's flat to explain the missing items? If not, did she know her murderer and does this explain the missing photo album, perhaps containing incriminating photographs?

MURDOCH TERRACE, 1996

Map ref. 8

Turn right along Dundee Street to Murdoch Terrace where, on 26 April 1996, twenty-one-year-old Mandy Barnett, a nightclub worker, was murdered in her first-floor flat.

The police were alerted after Barnett's boyfriend, convicted killer thirty-nine-year-old John Balsillie, raised the alarm from his prison cell in Saughton. His regular phone call to Barnett had been answered by a man who refused to give his name but whom Balsillie recognised as the voice of Joseph McGinlay – a convicted killer and rapist who had presumably used his acquaintance with Balsillie to get access to Barnett's home. Redialling repeatedly produced only the engaged tone and, when Barnett failed to turn up for her usual prison visit that evening, Balsillie was alarmed and reported his fears to a prison officer. He phoned a friend of Barnett's and asked her to check her address. The friend got no reply.

With a key from Balsillie, the police found the phone off the hook and signs of disturbance in the living room. Checking the rest of the flat led to the grim discovery of Barnett's body. Partially clothed in T-shirt and underwear, she was lying in a bloodstained bath. She had been brutally attacked, stabbed and murdered. As the door of her flat had not been forced, it seemed that she had known her killer and that the prime suspect was the man who had been in the flat when Balsillie had telephoned.

Balsillie had been jailed for life in 1976 after murdering an eighty-two-year-old woman during a break-in at her home in the Gracemount area. Let out on parole in 1993, he had been sent back to jail three years later in April 1996 – the month of Mandy's killing – after being convicted of another city break-in. He claimed that he had been looking for cash after blowing his unemployment benefit on a Valentine's Day treat for his girlfriend, who had just started working in the Subway Club in the Cowgate as a cloakroom attendant. She spoke to Balsillie every day on the telephone.

Barnett had had little contact with her family since moving to Edinburgh three years previously. An attractive young woman with short cropped auburn hair, a nose stud and a Cockney accent, she spent much of her spare time clubbing in nearby Wilkie House. Her six-year-old daughter, meanwhile, lived with relatives in Luton, Bedfordshire.

A blue Rover Metro, which had bumped into a stolen car reported to the police and discovered near the flat where Barnett lived, together with other evidence inside the flat, led to the arrest of Joseph McGinlay. When Balsillie had gone there with the police a week later, he said that the television and two large kitchen knives were missing, and that the bloodstains on the carpet had not been there when he had visited for the last time before being sent back to prison earlier that month.

The bloodstained footprint at the front door, which a policeman had covered with a lid, was tracked down by police. The detectives were interested in a particular style marketed through Freeman Hardy and Willis outlets and a pair sold in a shop in Forfar in March 1995. When McGinlay was questioned about shoes, he complained about how difficult it was to get a good fit and that he had thrown away a pair which had become bloodstained after rubbing all the skin off his heels. He then told the police that Barnett had been killed by a local dealer who, when approached, admitted selling ecstacy to Mandy and also stealing the ghetto-blaster (and, presumably, the TV) from her home as she owed him £60. The dealer also admitted that he was in Murdoch Terrace only twenty yards away on the day she died, but denied killing her and said he was there to see a friend.

Meanwhile, evidence revealed forty-year-old Joseph McGinlay as a scheming psychopath, sex offender and one of Scotland's longest-serving murderers, who had spent twenty-two years behind bars before finally convincing prison psychiatrists that he could be trusted with freedom – only to kill again.

Prison psychologists had assessed McGinlay as a devious man with no feeling for others. But the authorities proceeded with a series of unsupervised visits – despite the advice of psychologists whose courses he attended on anger management – and granted him the hours of freedom which would end with the death of Barnett.

Barnett's parents appealed for an investigation into how their daughter's killer came to be free, despite his horrific record for violence. Alistair Darling, MP for Edinburgh Central, also called for an investigation into how such a convicted killer could slip through the prison security net designed to prevent dangerous criminals being granted home leave, declaring that 'the Scottish Prison Sevice's duty to rehabilitate should not outweigh public safety'. A local hotelier had already claimed that he had unwittingly employed a double killer and rapist to work in the grounds of his hotel under a prison work-placement scheme. Noranside Open Prison, near Forfar, was to review its arrangements after it was revealed that a convicted sex offender had been placed at a council residential home. Angus Council also complained that McGinlay had been sent to work at Fairlie House, an old peoples' home in Kirriemuir, in breach of an agreement that no one convicted of such offences should be sent on placement to social work premises.

As part of his training for freedom, McGinlay was on his third weekend leave from Noranside, having been transferred there when he was reclassified as a category D prisoner. Prisoners are assessed by the hall manager and the governor, but the decision to lower a prisoner's category lies ultimately with the Secretary of State for Scotland. Only category D convicts at open prisons are eligible for home leave.

Expecting to be released in July 1997, McGinlay had only fifteen months left to serve. In February 1996 the resettlement team decided to offer him home leave accommodation in a council-run hostel for offenders. Despite his horrific record, they had arranged for him to spend two weekends at a hostel in Edinburgh's city centre in March. He was given his first weekend pass later that month. A fortnight later he was permitted a second pass. Each time he was allowed to roam free through Edinburgh between the hours of 8 a.m. and 11 p.m.

Despite breaking strict curfew rules and returning drunk to the sixteen-bed hostel, he was allowed that fateful third unescorted weekend four weeks later. Within hours of his arrival in the city on Friday, 26 April, he had killed Mandy Barnett.

Hostel staff admitted they had noticed a change in his character on that last stay. They knew he seemed a bit different. He arrived, dropped off his belongings, maybe changed his clothes and took off. He kept an appointment with his supervising social worker at midday, but thereafter was not in contact until he arrived back at the hostel at 11.30 p.m., half an hour after curfew. It was immediately observed that he had been drinking, but the next day there was no indication that anything major was wrong with his behaviour until he was booked by police on the Saturday afternoon.

Questioned, he began weaving an intricate web of lies about the suspected drug-pusher to throw off the police. Later he admitted these were only to protect his hopes of release.

Evidence of an earlier victim emerged at McGinlay's trial. In 1974 Josie Fraser was just thirteen years old when McGinlay – seventeen and already a convicted sex attacker sent down for two years for attempted rape of a forty-year-old Ayrshire neighbour in

1972 – struck her with an iron bar and a knife before murdering her sixteen-year-old friend outside a derelict flat in Glasgow's Charing Cross where his parents once lived. McGinlay then dragged the unconscious Fraser into the house and thrust her into a wardrobe. Minutes from death, a passing policeman heard her sobs.

McGinlay – nicknamed Alvin Stardust because he always wore black clothes and leather gloves like the pop star – was well known locally but not well liked. Josie Fraser, returning to consciousness, whispered, 'The gloves'. Her relatives sought the teenage killer but he had already been arrested, despite washing blood off himself in the River Kelvin. Twenty-two years later, the Parole Board were convinced he could be safely released and sent to Noranside Open Prison.

McGinlay was sentenced to a second term of imprisonment for life. His name will now be added to the short but infamous list of murderers in Scotland who have been reprieved but who, on their release, have murdered again. In 1958 Donald 'Ginger' Forbes had been sentenced to death for the murder of a night watchman in Granton. Reprieved after serving just under twelve years of a life sentence before being freed on licence in 1970, within eight weeks he had stabbed a man to death in a brawl and received a second life sentence. In 1967 George Emslie murdered a neighbour in Crosshill, Fife, with a shotgun. He was paroled after ten years, but in 1992 he axed his brother to death and received a second life sentence.

Perhaps even more remarkable, however, is the story of Donald Merrett, the Edinburgh student who, in 1926, shot his mother in Buckingham Terrace and was released on a 'not proven' verdict, only to return nearly twenty years later with devastating results (*see* p. 76).

TOLCROSS AND LOTHIAN ROAD

ANNABEL'S DISCO, SEMPLE STREET, 1984

Map ref. 9

From Murdoch Terrace return along Dundee Street to Fountainbridge and Semple Street where, on 27 April 1984, nineteen-year-old Pauline Reilly was strangled at Annabel's Disco. She was found by her father, 'Paddy' Reilly, when he called in to see her at 6.40 p.m. that evening and restock the bar.

Murder squad detectives immediately tried to trace two men in their early twenties 'of swarthy appearance' – possibly from the Middle East – and described as slim. One was about 5'6" tall, with dark frizzy collar-length hair and wearing a dark jacket and jeans. His companion was about two inches taller, with a hooked nose and black frizzy hair, wearing a three-quarter-length light raincoat.

Both men had been observed two hours before, at about 4.30 p.m. that Friday evening, standing at the Semple Street doorway as if they were waiting to get into the office. A dark car with distinctive white walled tyres and three occupants had been seen parked nearby at about 4 p.m. Fifteen minutes later it was seen again parked around the corner in Morrison Street.

Pauline Reilly, a former pupil at George Heriot's, ran the disco as day manageress. Since leaving school in the summer of 1983, she had worked in the office taking telephone calls and dealing with advance bookings. Her father had last seen her alive at lunchtime that day when he had gone to the office to sign pay cheques. Her dog was with her at the time. Reilly said that he had often warned Pauline in the past not to work there with the door of the safe open as it was quite normal for people to come to the office door and knock for admission.

Pauline's aunt, who did some cleaning at the disco, said that as she was leaving at 3.25 p.m., Pauline had told her she would be back at her flat in Gardner's Crescent only a short walk away at 4.30 p.m. But when Pauline's boyfriend phoned at about 4.45 p.m., she had not yet arrived.

On the day Pauline died there was no one else in the office, but outside it was a busy Friday afternoon in that part of Edinburgh with a lot of traffic and passers-by. Reilly, a local businessman, offered a £5000 reward for information leading to the arrest and conviction of his daughter's killer or killers. Pauline's sister Dawn – aged twenty-one and the night manageress of the disco – refused to return as the memory was too painful.

Over £3000 was found to be missing from the safe. The motive seemed to be robbery and Pauline had been strangled with a rope made of sash cord wound three times around her throat – her body left partially suspended from a spiral staircase. As there was no sign of a struggle, the police pathologist suggested that she had been standing when the rope was applied from behind. She would have lost consciousness within seconds and death would have taken place in six minutes.

There was no sign of a forced entry to the premises but anyone in a car or on a bus at the traffic lights at the Fountainbridge–Semple Street junction would be able to see into the doorway of the office on the corner of the building. Evidence suggested that there was a strong possibility that Pauline knew her killer.

It was a piece of paper with the name, address and telephone number of Shu-Kee Leung, employed as a waiter at the Dragonara Hotel, found in Pauline's office which led to his arrest on suspicion of murder. Asked how it got there, Leung said that on the day of the murder he was at home in Warrender Park Crescent until 4.30 p.m., when he left to go to work. He had walked to Tollcross through Pontin Street and along Fountainbridge into Gardner's Crescent.

Denying all knowledge of the piece of paper, he claimed that it was possible his wife Norah might know something about it. She had formerly worked as a barmaid at the disco and after she left in August 1983 remained a frequent visitor. He also denied threatening Pauline with a knife stolen from the Dragonara Hotel and strangling her.

On the day after the murder Leung had boasted to a fellow waiter that he had won £2000 at a casino. Lahmamsi said, 'Leung was very excited about winning the money and when I said I did not believe it he showed me some of it.'

The manager of the Royal Chimes Casino in Royal Terrace said Leung was a regular but small gambler who would make £50 bets at a time. He had called perhaps three or four times a week for the last three years.

The manager also said his staff were trained to look out for people wanting to launder money at the casino – changing cash into chips, then later cashing in the chips for exactly the same amount and leaving the 'hot' money there. If a stranger came in with a large amount of money they would wonder why and treat it with caution, but not if this was a regular customer they were dealing with. He added that members of the Chinese community were fond of gambling. Very few of them drank and gambling was their main pastime.

On the Sunday after Pauline's murder Leung was in the casino and the waiter noticed the unusual size and type of bet he was placing – about £200 a time in cash. A croupier on duty a few days after had also cashed in chips worth £2000 for him in £100 notes.

Leung was asked by the police to provide specimens of his handwriting since there was a fingerprint from his left hand on the scrap of paper in Pauline's office. As he was doing this Leung became quite agitated and the inspector suspected that he was trying to disguise his writing. It was this evidence, as well as information that he was in trouble financially and had debts of £1000, which led to his arrest – accused of strangling Pauline Reilly and robbing her of £3,123.

At the trial her father denied that he had put out a £30,000 contract on Leung – a rumour that had gone round the town and reached the prison. He also said he knew of no one who would want to murder his daughter: she was very popular with disco goers. But he agreed that, during his time in the competitive disco business, he could have made friends and admitted to 'maybe some enemies'.

At his trial Leung said that he was forced 'by gangsters' to hang up Pauline's body. But he denied murdering her and said that she was already dead when he entered Annabel's Disco, taken there by a Mr Hasin – a recent acquaintance from an Edinburgh casino who, when Leung had lost all his money in late March or early April, had twice loaned him £10.

Leung claimed he later repaid £10 of the money he owed but, on the afternoon of the murder, Hasin phoned asking for the remaining money and a meeting was arranged outside a cinema near the disco. When Hasin arrived, Leung gave him the money and was offered a lift to Annabel's Disco.

The door was opened by a man in a white T-shirt and Leung saw a girl lying in the middle of the room.

'I see this guy walk to the corner near the window and he was putting a pair of white gloves on. I was really shocked and did not know what to do. I asked them, "What happened to the girl?", and they said, "We killed her and that's what we do for a living."'

Leung added that they told him that they wanted to get him involved, to be one of them in the future, and said it was easy work with lots of money. When he said he wanted to go and would not tell anyone about the murdered girl, the man in the T-shirt said, 'You don't think we would let you go just like that.'

He produced a gun and said they knew where Leung's wife and child lived. When Leung told them he had separated from his wife and two children earlier that year, they said if he did not do as he was told he would have his head blown off.

He was told to write down his name and address and did so. He was then told to move the body to the stairs and to hang her up.

'I was that frightened. I can't even think why they wanted me to hang her up for she is dead already. It doesn't make sense at all. But I just wanted to get out – get it over with.'

As Leung did as he was told, he said he was photographed as 'just a little guarantee'. The man in the T-shirt then gave him £500 and a bag of coins and Leung had no choice but to take them. After they left the disco Hasin and a third man, the driver of a car parked nearby, took him to his work at the Dragonara.

Next day Hasin phoned and Leung was taken to a flat in Tolcross where the man with the T-shirt said that a knife from Leung's hotel and a piece of paper with his name and address on it had been left in the disco office. Leung asked them if they were putting the blame on him and was told it would be enough to get the attention of the police and give them time to get away.

Leung told the sheriff he had decided to confess because he had been arrested and was awaiting trial while they were still free. 'They are gangsters. They would do anything they would think is necessary.' He added that, if he was cleared of the murder, he would have to flee the country because he was in fear of his life from the girl's killers. They would stop at nothing. He also maintained that he had eventually decided to tell the truth when, awaiting trial in prison, he had heard the rumour that the girl's father had put out a contract for £30,000 on his life.

He had gambling winnings of between £3000 and £4000 and had hidden more than £2000 in his car in the hotel car park, as he thought it would be the safest place. When he had given the police the keys, they found a small wallet containing £3200 in the boot. Removing the handbrake cover revealed another £200.

Leung denied a suggestion that he had made up his story about the gangsters when he realised that forensic evidence proved conclusively that he had been in the disco that day. His wife, called as a witness, declined to give evidence.

Leung, who was from Hong Kong, had previous minor convictions and was on deferred sentence for theft at the time of the murder. After a seven-day trial the jury by a majority verdict found him guilty of Pauline's murder. He was sent to prison for life.

Loose ends still remain, however. Were the mysterious Hasin and gangsters the men seen outside the disco two hours before Pauline's death? According to the pathologists, she was standing when the rope was drawn around her neck, whilst Leung claimed that she was already dead when he was forced to hang her body up. Even if that was the case, would he have been able to hang up a body – whether dead or alive – on his own? If alive, why had Pauline been so passive about her murder? And if dead, why hang up the body at all? Could it have been as a warning? And if so, for whom? And what about her dog? Had it any place in this scenario of violent death?

7 CHALMERS STREET, 1972

Map ref. 10

A short walk away from Tolcross and, in a street across from the Meadows, a hundred yards from Edinburgh Royal Infirmary, nineteen-year-old Janis Robertson was found murdered on 15 September 1972.

She had been strangled, and the discovery was made by two friends who had called at the second-floor room in the two-storey terraced villa at 7 Chalmers Street which housed several self-contained flatlets. The men immediately contacted the police. Detectives using light from a powerful generator searched the building for clues while two uniformed officers stood guard outside.

Robertson had worked in an Edinburgh shoe shop for some time before going back to her old job as a waitress, where she worked in the Kingfisher Restaurant in Bread Street, not far from the murder scene. One of her close friends, Annette McGowan – who worked in a Morningside restaurant as a trainee manageress – had known her for years. They had been out together earlier on that fatal Thursday night and were to meet again the following day.

Robertson's home address was given as Stenhouse Avenue West, where she lived with her mother and other members of her family. When she didn't return home that Thursday night as expected, they thought she had stayed at a friend's house.

The restaurant owner told the police that Robertson had worked there for about two weeks, although she had worked with them before for six months over a year ago and was a very pleasant girl – a good worker, a good-looking girl and very easy to get along with. When she did not turn up for work and they then heard of her death, it was a great shock.

The owner of 7 Chalmers Street had rented the room to a young man. She had several subdivided properties with self-contained flats, but much of the other property in the street, which overlooks the Meadows, was used as hospital offices.

Robertson was found lying half on a bed with a ligature tied very tightly around her neck. The vital clue was a ring found in her hair. It belonged to Walter Howden, aged twenty-eight, in whose room she had been found.

Howden was accused of punching and murdering her, despite an alibi that at the alleged time of her death between 6.15 and 6.35 p.m. he was on his way to and from a café.

According to a fifteen-year-old witness, Keith Black, it emerged that, several hours before her death, Robertson had tattooed Howden's hands with a cup, a cross and the words 'Mum and Dad', and had then begun a tattoo on his own arm in the café where she worked.

'She started the letter "K" then I spilled some ink and I had to wipe it up. I finished the tattoo myself.' He added that when he left the café at about 5 p.m. Howden and Robertson were still there. Another witness who lived in the house said that shortly after 6 p.m. he had met Howden on the stair. Howden had said he had a woman in his room but was not worried about being found out by the landlady who did not approve. Less than an hour later her body was found with a strip of linen tied tightly around her neck.

A friend of Robertson, Ronald Armstrong – who 'with some friends were more or less squatting' in one room in 9 Chalmers Street – said that Howden had raised the alarm. He had gone to Armstrong's room and said that they'd better go to no. 7 'because Janis is either dead or dying'.

Taken into custody and accused of Robertson's murder, Howden told detectives, 'I can't remember. I suffer from blackouts. I just remember seeing her at the table with papers from my anorak pockets. I can't remember what happened after that.' He said that a bottle of ink had spilled on Robertson's leg in the café and he had suggested they went to his flat to clean up. He had left the flat with Janis sitting on the bed. When he had come back she was still sitting there with her back to the window and blood coming from her nose.

Detectives found very little sign of any struggle in the room and during the four-day trial the jury was told that Robertson had been strangled with a strip of linen torn from a pillow case wound very tightly round her neck. A heavy ring, worn by the accused, was entangled in her hair beside the ligature. This had led to Howden's arrest, but he denied the charge, accusing the police of planting the ring.

A psychiatrist called for the defence said that in his opinion, if Howden had murdered the girl, he would be suffering from diminished responsibility at the time. Howden admitted a number of previous convictions for assault and was jailed for life for Janis Robertson's murder.

THE USHER HALL,
LOTHIAN ROAD, 1986

Map ref. 11

A fight that would have done credit to the gangs in *West Side Story* took place near the Usher Hall on the night of 7 March 1986. One man died and two others were in hospital – one with severe chest wounds; another with severe head injuries.

All the victims were from Edinburgh and the police embarked on a hunt for a vicious killer. The man they were looking for was between 25 and 30, 5'8" and slim, with bushy wiry shoulder-length hair, dark and unkempt, and a bushy beard. He was also described as having a black eye. It seemed he had been in trouble before the incident.

There were lots of cars and people about that evening and as a result of their inquiries, twenty-three-year-old John Forbes came forward. He stated that the man they were looking for was Andrew Sinclair, a friend of his, and that they had been ambushed by youths as they were crossing Lothian Road towards the Usher Hall. They both ran away and were followed by one member of the gang who jumped on Sinclair.

Forbes dragged Sinclair away and then saw that his friend was holding a knife. He realised Sinclair had used it and was very upset.

At his trial Sinclair – aged twenty-five and unemployed, but having previously worked as a residential care officer in an assessment centre – said that he had been on his way home when the incident occured. He had been drinking heavily and was crossing Lothian Road towards the Usher Hall, walking fairly briskly as he needed the toilet but Forbes was lagging behind a bit. As they pushed their way through a group of youths walking ahead, there had been 'an exchange of words'.

Nearing the Usher Hall he heard footsteps behind him and turned round to be punched in the head by one of the youths, Iain Laing. Sinclair claimed that he squared up to Laing and said he did not want any trouble. One of Laing's companions joined the fray and blows were exchanged.

Sinclair said he then turned and ran towards Grindlay Street, followed by the two youths who caught up with him. He turned to face them and, aware of his danger, took from his pocket a knife which he used to clean out his pipe and cut tobacco.

'I was in a state of near panic. I thought by bringing out the knife, I might be able to discourage these people from attacking me any more.' He made a couple of jabbing motions and did not know if he had struck Laing, who was halted in his tracks. 'That was as much as I wanted to happen.' He then felt a kick from behind and again jabbed the knife forward, catching one of the youths in the chest. Then he saw an arm coming down to 'club' him, so he raised his hand with the knife still in it and caught another of the youths.

Sinclair was unaware that anyone had been seriously injured, but when the police came to his house the next morning and said someone had died, 'My legs just about went from under me.'

He had originally told the police that one of the youths had come at him with a knife, but this was a lie. He later admitted he did not know what he was thinking about when he said it.

The jury took seventy-five minutes to find Andrew Sinclair not guilty of murdering Paul Gibson, aged twenty, who died from a single wound to the heart. Sinclair lodged a special plea of self-defence. He was also found not guilty of attempting to murder

Iain Laing, aged twenty, by stabbing him on the body and of striking Keith Halliday, also aged twenty, on the arm with a knife.

Sinclair was acquitted of the murder charge, but was found guilty of breach of the peace in Lothian Road that night. He admitted a further breach of the peace in Cowgate on 28 February, and was released on condition that he lived in his father's house in Leopold Place.

THE NEW TOWN

31 BUCKINGHAM TERRACE, 1926 AND 22 MONTPELIER ROAD, 1954

Map refs 12 and 12a

From Lothian Road, cross over Princes Street and go down Queensferry Street over Dean Bridge to Buckingham Terrace, an elegant, tree-lined, shopless cul-de-sac with the air of gentility of a forgotten age. This imposing row of tall mid-Victorian houses had by the early years of the twentieth century lost something of its grandeur. As well as nobly bearing the shame of a few discreet and moderately expensive guest houses, some of its houses were being quietly converted into flats for gentlefolk, particularly widows and retired businessmen.

Buckingham Terrace was a place for snobs, typified by the notorious Morningside epithet, 'Fur coats and nae knickers', and in 1926 it possessed all the right ingredients to attract Mrs Bertha Merrett, daughter of a prosperous wine merchant from Manchester who, in 1907, had married a New Zealand engineer.

The following year their only son Donald was born. They travelled to Russia and there John Merrett deserted his wife and child, although she maintained the pretence of being a war widow.

At least Mrs Merrett had no financial worries, having been left comfortably off to the tune of £700 per annum by her father, and she was immensely proud of her tall handsome son. But she was aware that, even aged sixteen, Donald did not always tell the truth and that sometimes he stole money from her purse – which of course he hotly denied.

Ambitious for her darling, she sent him to Malvern College. It was a disaster. He hated the discipline and, when he rebelled against it, she saw that her dream of him going on to Oxford University would have to be abandoned.

Although she pretended not to notice the shortcomings of his nature, trying to convince herself that he was just full of boyish pranks which he would outgrow given time, she was sensible to the temptations offered by having too much freedom; temptations which might successfully be kept at bay by sending him to a university where he could live at home under her watchful eye. Edinburgh was the obvious choice and, in readiness for Donald enrolling as a student, she took lodgings in Palmerston Place in 1926 before moving into a small but adequately elegant converted drawing-room flat at 31 Buckingham Terrace.

Mrs Merrett's hopes were soon dashed. Donald hated lectures, hated study even more, and games made him tired. He wasn't popular and he was always short of cash, vociferously despising the ten shillings a week his mother allowed him and which were less than adequate for his favourite haunt, the Dunedin Palais de Dance at Picardy Place. There flashy young men could daringly book out a 'young lady' for thirty shillings for an evening and fifteen shillings for the afternoon, in lieu of the dances she was missing. As transport was a necessity for these jaunts, Donald put down £26 for a motor bike and the more sinister purchase of a snub-nosed Japanese pistol.

Now desperate for money, he discovered the simple answer was to forge his mother's name on cheques by tracing her signature in pencil and then inking it in. The bank clerks he dealt with paid it over in good faith. Even if there was a budding Sherlock Holmes in their midst, it was probably more than his job was worth to hint that an Edinburgh student – the only son of a well-off widow who was devoted to his mother – was capable of such an offence.

In two months Donald had absorbed over £200, a third of his mother's yearly income. Nemesis was at hand, however, when Mrs Merrett paid the landlord the balance of her rent and a letter from the bank arrived on the morning of 17 March 1926. To her astonishment, she read that her account was now overdrawn.

If there had been words between mother and son, the maid Rita was not aware of them as she cleared away the breakfast dishes. Donald was reading a book in an armchair and his mother was a few feet away preparing to write letters once the table was cleared.

A few moments later she heard a loud bang and the sound of falling books, and Donald rushed into the kitchen.

'My mother has shot herself,' he said.

When Rita exclaimed why should she do such a thing, Donald replied that he had been wasting his mother's money and he thought she was worried about that.

They found her, still breathing, lying on the floor between the table and the bureau, on the top of which lay a pistol that the maid had never seen before. Donald, meanwhile, phoned the police and suggested to Rita that they go down and wait for the ambulance to take his mother to the hospital.

Two policemen arrived. Decent, deferential men, suitably chastened by such an appalling domestic tragedy, they were prepared to believe every word. After all, this wasn't some hovel down a High Street close or the nasty slums of Leith Walk, this was a nice respectable neighbourhood. Decent law-abiding folk lived here, pillars of Edinburgh society, so instead of regarding the circumstances as suspicious and asking searching questions, they began to 'tidy up', setting the room to rights, regardless of possible fingerprints on the pistol. In William Roughhead's oft-quoted words in his account of the trial: the pair 'might have been competent for a part in the "Policemen's Chorus" in *The Pirates of Penzance.'*

The ambulance arrived to take Mrs Merrett to the Royal

Infirmary. There she was to suffer the further indignity of being confined to a security ward with barred windows as a potential suicide risk. Donald followed her. She was still alive.

'So it's still on the cards that she will recover,' he said to the nurse, telling her that his mother had no friends in Edinburgh (which was untrue) and that she didn't get on with her sisters (another lie), so it was no use calling any of them. He then took himself off to the Palais de Dance, and took his lady friend off for a spin down to Queensferry.

When he returned, his mother was conscious, dazed and bewildered since nobody could tell her what had happened except that she had had 'a little accident'. When asked for her account of the little accident she said, 'I was sitting writing at the table and my son Donald was standing beside me. I said, "Go away, Donald, and don't annoy me." And the next I heard was a kind of explosion. Suddenly a bang went off in my head and I don't remember any more.' Various inconsistent, confused statements followed. To her sister Mrs Penn – who disproved Donald's allegations by anxiously rushing up from England to be at Bertha's bedside – Mrs Merrett said it was, 'as if Donald had shot me'. But she did not really believe that and added, 'He is such a naughty boy.'

When Mrs Penn asked Donald to explain, he merely shrugged and said, 'No, Auntie, I did not do it, but if you like I will confess.'

He didn't, of course, nor did he allow his mother's condition to affect his life, apart from moving into a hotel on Lothian Road. The cheque book was now his, and he made the most of it while his mother still breathed, drawing out £156 over the following nine days, including the down payment on a racing motorbike.

His mother's death from basal meningitis on 27 March brought his career as a forger to a halt. His aunt and uncle came to stay in Buckingham Terrace to look after him, perhaps with some compassion for his mother's 'suicide', the verdict accepted by the police.

Mrs Merrett's will had taken the unusual step of entrusting the management of her estate and the guardianship of her son to the Public Trustee. Perhaps she was unsure of the willingness of her sisters to take care of her boy or had secret doubts about his emotional condition.

The Public Trustee, preparatory to a decision on the boy's future, had him medically examined: 'Exceptionally developed physically for his age and looks at least over twenty years. He talks intelligently and confidently, and is clear and lucid in his statements on general topics . . . mentally he is perfectly sane.' Donald should have been able to breathe freely at last, but there was still the little matter of the investigation into Mrs Merrett's finances necessary for probate.

And Donald was undone. They wanted to know why this careful woman had suddenly embarked on such expenditure in the last three months before her death? And, most surprising of all, how could a woman lying at death's door – confined in a hospital suicide ward – have signed cheques for £150, to say nothing of buying a racing motorbike?

Police interest revived remarkably at these disclosures. Donald was arrested in December 1926 and charged with murder and forgery. The trial began in the following February. But as it was almost a year after his mother's death, the maid Rita's evidence was confused and conflicting. Other evidence was also shaky. There was discussion about the pistol and the position of the head wound was arguable so the jury was left to decide.

Was it likely that, because of an argument over money, a devoted son would take up a pistol and shoot his doting mother? She might have been shocked to hear that he had been forging her cheques, but was that just cause for him to blow her brains out?

Donald had arrived at court wearing a huge felt brimmed hat, horn-rimmed Harold Lloyd spectacles (which were very fashionable), a loose collar and no tie. According to the press, he showed 'a smiling unconcern' as he lied with the frequency and ease of long practice.

The jury were out for only fifty-five minutes and fell back on that most useful of Scottish verdicts: 'Not proven' – which those of a cynical nature have long interpreted as: 'We know you did it, go away, and don't do it again.'

But that was exactly what Donald Merrett did.

Sent down for twelve months on the forgery charge, which he greeted with 'stoical calm', he celebrated his freedom by embarking on a new life. Under the assumed name of Chesney, he went to stay with Mary Bonnar, Lady Menzies, an old friend of his mother's. She was wealthy and he eloped with her favourite daughter, seventeen-year-old Vera, whom he married in a Glasgow registrar's office.

When he came of age, he inherited £50,000 from his maternal grandfather. At last the world he had longed for was his: fast cars, beautiful women, playboys and gamblers. He bought a twenty-room mansion, a Bentley and a private plane. His sleek yacht was a common sight on the Mediterranean where, in 1936, he dabbled in smuggling and gun-running to Franco's Spain.

By now the well-developed teenage Edinburgh student who murdered his mother was a huge man weighing 22 stones, with a thick black beard, a gold earring and bracelet. But his impressive appearance was no match for the seasoned gamblers on the Riviera. His fortune evaporated and just in time he made an £8500 settlement on his wife Vera, which he was later to regret and declare 'a mental aberration'.

But there was method in his madness. The endowment would revert to him upon her death and it was this clause which was eventually to lead to her murder.

The Second World War saw him commissioned, earning the nickname 'Crasher Chesney' after piling up three torpedo boats. Totally without fear, he waded single-handedly towards the advancing Germans at Tobruk, spraying them with machine-gun fire, and in post-War Germany his reputation reached almost mythical proportions when he stole three lorryloads of army rifles and ferried them across the border to East German black marketeers.

The War ended in 1945 but not his reputation. No longer a hero, he found himself a marked man with Interpol at his heels. With his profitable smuggling days drawing swiftly to a close, his thoughts turned to his estranged wife Vera whom he had abandoned in Scotland some years earlier, and in particular to that endowment he had settled on her. With a plan looming large in his mind, he returned to Edinburgh and on 21 January 1954 took Vera, now an alcoholic, on a massive pub crawl, establishing that they were on the best of terms. He told her that he was soon to emigrate to a new life in New Zealand.

Returning to Germany on 8 February, he told his mistress Sonia, 'Pack your bags. We're going on holiday to Amsterdam.' There he plotted to put a daring plan into effect. On their second night he briefly interrupted the holiday and returned to Scotland. He was gone for one night only. A business deal had come up, was the story he told Sonia.

Shaving off his beard and removing the earring, he combed back his hair and put on a pair of horn-rimmed glasses. Walking with a limp, he boarded the evening flight to Edinburgh with a forged passport . . . to keep his date with murder.

His destination was in the Bruntsfield area – 22 Montpelier Road – where Vera ran a guest house for retired gentlefolk. It was a cold February night while he watched from across the street until the light went on in her bedroom. He then vaulted the fence and made straight for the French windows. A faulty catch had not been mended and he was inside.

The dogs knew him and greeted him as he made his way up the stairs and entered the bedroom. Vera was seated at her dressing-table and he knew at once she had been drinking. He felt no pity for this sad wreck of a woman he had briefly loved long ago, whose eyes lit up at the sight of two bottles of duty free gin he held up.

As they drank together he watched her, awaiting his opportunity – callously deciding that the world would be better off without her and carefully avoiding questions about the divorce and the £8500 he had settled on her.

Half an hour later Vera had passed out, and she did not move as he carried her into the adjoining bathroom and watched until the tub slowly filled. She did not stir as he carefully lowered her into the tepid water and her head slid silently under.

Preparing to leave by the way he had entered the house, he had bargained without the possibility that his mother-in-law, Lady Menzies, was visiting. She barred his way. They struggled and he seized a heavy coffee pot and crushed her skull with it.

He still had a chance, he thought. As far as the police were concerned, he was on holiday in Amsterdam and he believed he could prove it. He was wrong. That last fatal meeting with Lady Menzies had destroyed all his carefully laid plans.

John Donald Chesney was still Merrett. The Merrett who had murdered his mother had returned to Edinburgh to murder two more victims. Scotland Yard was on the case. So was Interpol.

He returned to the dark cobbled streets of Cologne to the house where he had been living with Sonia before the disastrous trip to Amsterdam. She had also deserted him.

With nowhere to run to, he took one last taxi ride out into the German countryside. There, in a lonely wood beneath the stars, he placed the barrel of his Colt 45 in his mouth and took his own life. With the same cold efficiency he had shown to his other three victims.

NOTE: The first part of the Merrett murder, before he became John Donald Chesney, has been reported extensively in William Roughhead's *Trials* and in Allan Massie's excellent *Ill Met by Gaslight* (Paul Harris/Futura 1980).

11B BUCKINGHAM TERRACE, 1993

Map ref. 12

Move the calendar foward forty years to 1993. Buckingham Terrace has many more guest houses, and most of the elegant houses whose owners used to live in style with a staff of servants have been transformed into expensive flats. Ronald Tripp lived in one of them, a basement flat at no. 11.

His brother James, calling on 8 October, could get no reply from the front door. Walking round, he peered into the window. Sixty-five-year-old Ronald was lying on the floor.

James' first thought was that he had had a heart attack. The police were called and forced an entry. What they found was far worse. Ronald was dead. He had been struck thirty times on the head, his skull shattered in a frenzied attack.

'It was a terrible shock,' said James. 'I still can't believe it. Ronnie was such a trusting man, perhaps too trusting.'

As there was no sign of a break-in and robbery did not appear to be a motive, the immediate suspicion was that Tripp had known his killer. Once the police looked into the private life of the dead man, their inquiries quickly led them to the prime suspect.

Philip Brummitt, aged thirty-seven and an odd job man for a shop in Dalry Road, had agreed to do some electrical work in Tripp's flat and was given £17 for installing an extra socket. Two days later a neighbour heard loud noises from the basement.

On the face of it Brummitt, a Falklands veteran, had battered his victim to death for a few pounds. But he would do all he could to make sure that what happened just before the murder did not come out in court.

'It is either talk to you or a priest, isn't it?' he said to the police. 'I thought he had money and I went to rob him and it just got totally out of hand. I do not know what came over me. I got about £20. That's what the stupid part is. I went to rob him, he had a go at me and I hit him with the hammer.'

Brummitt had joined the Army at twenty-one and served in Germany, Ireland and the Falklands. He had left after nine years with an exemplary service record. Prior to the murder, however, he had amassed what were to him monstrous debts of £600–700. Having already been to Tripp's home, he had realised there was cash in the flat and on the day of the killing had said to Tripp, 'I want your money.' There had been a struggle and Brummitt was suddenly aware of hitting Tripp with a hammer he had taken to the flat in his toolbag. He did not know how often he had struck his victim, only that he took £20 and left.

But there was more to it than that.

Tripp lived a quiet life in the flat he rented from the Links Housing Association. One of eleven children, he had returned to Edinburgh to be nearer the surviving members of his family. Shopping at the supermarket, he would then pop into Murray's second-hand shop on Dalry Road, one of many dealers and charity shops throughout Edinburgh where Tripp was well known and always guaranteed a friendly welcome. And Murray's was where Brummitt worked.

Apart from the occasional whispered innuendo, there was nothing to suggest that the jolly man everyone liked had a secret. But evidence at the murder scene revealed that the retired shopkeeper had performed a sexual act with another man shortly before his death.

Had it not been for the forensic evidence which showed

Brummitt was not telling the whole truth, he could have got away with the lesser charge of culpable homicide. But two days after carrying out the work, Brummitt returned and had sex with the elderly man. He then used a hammer to kill him. Like his victim, Brummitt was not known to be gay and it is possible he was trying to blackmail Tripp by threatening to uncover his secret.

Brummitt refused to confirm this theory but was so desperate to keep his gay liaison secret that he agreed to plead guilty to murder when he feared the evidence would be revealed in court.

He was jailed for life.

4 JAMAICA STREET, 1923

Map ref. 13

Cross Dean Bridge to Randolph Crescent, Queen Street and down
Howe Street where no. 4 Jamaica Street no longer exists. The street
beyond no. 2a was demolished and rebuilt in the years of Edinburgh's architectural reconstruction as Jamaica Lanes North and
South.

Past its former glory Jamaica Street was still flourishing as
rather seedy tenements when on 23 June 1923 Philip Murray
(thirty-one) pushed William Ronald Cree (thirty) to his death out
of the upstairs window of no. 4.

Cree's desperate struggles were watched by neighbours
who refused to intervene. Mrs Catherine Donaghue – a widow
known as Kate or Katie Rose, whose home it was – turned
King's evidence and would walk from the witness box a free
woman.

Catherine had married John Donaghue, a soldier, in 1914. He
had deserted her and she had lived for two years in Jamaica Street
where she paid 14s 10d rent per month. She had met Murray in
Cockburn Street, they had got drunk together and, although he
moved in with her, he did not contribute any money to the house-
keeping.

Cree, of Dunfermline, was a railway surfaceman. Unmarried,
he had served in the Black Watch and had been wounded three
times. A strong man and in good health, he occasionally visited

Edinburgh on a Saturday afternoon for the football and returned home by the last train.

On that fatal Saturday he met Donaghue in a local pub and after a heavy drinking session she took him home with her. Her local reputation was well-known. One neighbour, observing her enter the house with Cree, remarked, 'Kitty's got another victim tonight.'

In the house Donaghue found Murray fully dressed in the bed. He heard her whispering to Cree, got up, butted Cree in the face with his head, and dragged him to the open window.

Cree tried to free himself, shouting, 'I never came to fight. I'll give you a drink.'

Murray replied, 'I do not want drink. How much money have you got?'

In answer, Cree tried to shake off Murray's grip and witnesses, who perhaps had little love for a local prostitute, maintained that Donaghue was also at the window, assisting Murray by striking Cree whose struggles were in vain. Clinging desperately to the ledge and screaming loudly, he was pushed out while Murray looked down at him and said, without a trace of remorse, 'If he had given me money, he wouldn't have been out there.'

The trial took place on 9 October. Donaghue said she had a fifteen-year-old daughter who resided with her. Asked what she did for a living, she said she was a prostitute and earned about £7 per week. Murray was living off her earnings and sometimes sold newspapers and diaries on the streets. On the day of the tragedy he had been singing on the street. Donaghue insisted that she had tried to get between the two men but Murray was also very drunk. The jury retired at 6 p.m. and returned twenty-seven minutes later with a majority verdict of 'guilty of murder' against Murray.

The judge donned the black cap and pronounced sentence. Murray was to be detained in prison in Edinburgh until 30 October. Between 8 a.m. and 10 a.m. that morning he was to be hanged by the neck until he was dead.

The silence which followed the judge's invocation to God to have mercy on the prisoner's soul was broken by the condemned man speaking in low but firm tones.

'I must thank my counsel for the defence on my behalf. I do not think it was very fair of the jury to accept Mrs Donaghue's evidence against me. I am fully prepared to meet my God. I never put that man through the window as is alleged against me. Thank you.'

The prisoner was conducted to the cells below while someone at the back of the court (with a macabre sense of humour) shouted, 'Cheer up, Phil!'

The Scotsman of 10 October carried the headline: 'Newsvendor condemned to die. Prisoner's protestation of innocence.'

And what about Donaghue? Did she have a hand in Cree's death as neighbours alleged and, if so, why? She had picked Cree up, perhaps in her line of business. Did she know Murray was in bed in the house when she took Cree home? Surely she would have expected trouble, or was robbery the motive? And how did Murray manage to throw Cree – described as 'a big strong railwayman, in good health' – single-handedly out of the window, especially if he was very drunk? Or was Cree even more drunk?

A Snapshot in Time

In June 1923 Edinburgh had a firm grip on the twentieth century and was rapidly establishing itself as a place of modern, exciting living. There were still two classes – the flat cap and the bowler – the streets were mainly cobbled, and Edinburgh was famed as a major publishing centre. Many of the poorer houses had a weekly bath night, but with no running water, it was still the tin tub placed in front of the kitchen fire.

As for shops, some are still there: the former James Thin's bookshop on South Bridge, (now part of the Ottakar's chain), Jenners of Princes Street and Wilkies in Shandwick Place – in those days

9 Torphichen Street where Ernest Dumoulin and Helga Konrad stayed (1972).

Portrait of a killer: Ernest Dumoulin (page 7).

Mr and Mrs Konrad, Helga's parents.

The Salisbury Crags – policemen searching for clues.

The Guest House Murder (1974): 13 Torphichen Street (page 26).

Annabel's Disco (1984): Pauline Reilly's murder (page 55).

Willy Merrilees 1909–94: the pocket-sized detective with the battleship reputation (page 121).

Ronald Tripp: battered to death (page 78).

Death in 11b Buckingham Terrace (1993) (page 77).

Phillip Brummitt: under arrest (page 78).

St Vincent's Bar (1982) (page 84).

Marshall's Court (page 89).

The World's End pub: murders still unsolved (page 113).

Police searching at Haddington where Helen Scott's body was found.

The Torso Murder (1969) (page 148).

The Murder Squad at work.

with tailormade suits and coats in velours, serges and tweeds from 4 guineas. Others are well within living memory: Forsyths, Darlings and Patrick Thomson's, advertised with a Parade of Living Models, where a woman could buy a reliable fur coat for 95 guineas. A bargain! As for motor cars, a Citroen four-seater could be purchased for £340 and an Armstrong Siddeley family tourer for £360. And the end of the household drudgery of sweeping, brushing and washing was signalled by a demonstration of a Hoover Electric Cleaner at Sibbald & Sons, Shandwick Place.

As for entertainment, Sir Forbes Robertson was giving a recital of *An Actor's View of Shakespeare* at the Music Hall, part of the Assembly Rooms in George Street, and the movies had come to town. The Princes Street Picture House at no. 131 was showing Anita Stewart in *A Question of Honour*, plus travel, comedy and other subjects of interest. And at no. 54 Princes Street the New Picture House invited patrons to see Dorothy Dalton in *The Crimson Challenge*, a picture of surpassing dramatic interest.

Meanwhile, in the national news, Lloyd George had received an acclaimed welcome in the United States, and Britain had taken to the air in, according to *The Scotsman*, 'the great maritime air event, the Schneider Cup, which had been won on *Shell Spirit* by Lt David Rittenhouse, USN, piloting a Curtis Navy Racer with an incredible speed of 177.4 m.p.h.'

ST VINCENT BAR,
ST VINCENT STREET, 1982

Map ref. 14

Turn left out of Jamaica Street along Howe Street to where it becomes St Vincent Street. There, in April 1982, Ron Lockhart, a male nurse and part-time barman at the St Vincent Bar, was shot in the back.

At 11.20 p.m. on Sunday night, 4 April, two masked men with sawn-off shotguns made off in a large dark-coloured car parked in Circus Lane near the side entrance to the bar.

The motive was thought to be another failed robbery, and Lockhart may have been killed when one of the shotguns went off accidentally. When the gunmen burst into the bar, Lockhart was playing a fruit machine. Two other barmen and a friend were all ordered into the toilet. There they heard a shot, silence and the sound of a car speeding away. Lockhart was found lying dead on the floor outside the toilet door and his killer was arrested on the evidence of his partner in crime.

John Wilson, aged eighteen, identified thirty-year-old Jimmy Baigrie, a petty thief, saying he was not putting all the blame on him just to get himself off the hook but that the robbery had been Baigrie's idea. He told the court that inside the bar he had been guarding the doors while Baigrie ordered Lockhart and the other staff into the toilet at gunpoint. He maintained that he was out of sight of the action and had heard 'a thump' but not a shot. In his evidence, Baigrie said that the shot was not loud because the gun went off when it touched Lockhart accidentally.

Wilson made a plea of not guilty to the murder, only to attempted robbery and expected a more lenient sentence than six years' detention. But eyewitnesses said that Wilson had been wearing a red mask during the raid and that it had been the man in the red mask who had ordered the bar staff into the toilet.

Wilson claimed they were mistaken. He said that Baigrie talked big. He liked nothing better than boasting in bars about his well-laid plans for armed robberies and daring wage snatches, as well as selling explosives to terrorists. All were apparently meticulously worked out to the last detail.

'But that's all it was,' claimed Wilson. 'All talk.'

According to Wilson, when Baigrie stormed into the St Vincent Bar, there was no sign of the ice-cold Mr Big. Instead, he seemed to go berserk, shrieking at the staff, ordering them about, wildly waving the shotgun around and hitting them viciously with it, before finally killing Lockhart. In contrast, his accomplice Wilson was the gullible dupe, drawn into the robbery with promises of an 'easy clean job' in which no one would be injured. Rich rewards were promised, and an escape to a life of luxury in Greece on the proceeds.

Wilson believed Baigrie's claims that they would get £30,000 from the bar hold-up. Instead, they fled empty-handed, on the run and leaving behind £250 in the open till.

Wilson, who came from a respectable family, was not long out of school when he had met Baigrie a few weeks before the robbery and fallen for his 'hard man' talk. Believing he was getting in tow with a big-time gangster, he was suitably impressed when Baigrie began carrying around a shotgun tied under his jacket. Even after the murder, it appeared Baigrie was undaunted. He would not shut up and went around various haunts in Fife boasting of his plans for a big wage snatch and trying to recruit a gang for the job.

In reality, he had led a life of petty crime, working for a spell as a craneman at Leith docks before trying the Army, with visions of getting into the Special Air Service. That lasted only three months and he bought himself out, went North and worked in the yards building oil production platforms at Nigg Bay and Ardersier. Various casual jobs followed before he returned to Edinburgh to clean up in a disco, returning to his home in Kelty where Wilson also lived.

Baigrie was always short of cash, spending it freely as soon as he got it on drink and flashy cars. But his need for money became urgent after a failed robbery attempt when he was caught by the police in his home in Kelty in August 1981 and charged with illegal possession of a shotgun and cartridges.

Due to appear for trial on this charge at Edinburgh Sheriff Court the following April, as the date approached he became more and more convinced that he would 'get time'. In a bid to escape the clutches of the law, he decided to rob the St Vincent Bar two weeks before the court case. This, he told Wilson, would give them both time to disappear to a life of luxury in Greece. He believed his plan was foolproof but he was wrong. It led not to a lifetime in a sunshine hideaway, but to a life sentence in a prison cell.

EAST END AND GREENSIDE

5 MARSHALL'S COURT, 1953

Map ref. 15

From St Vincent Street, Howe Street, go along Queen Street and York Place towards Leith Walk and Greenside. In the 1950s this was an area of narrow streets branching out into numerous courts and openings which ran steeply up the busy thoroughfare of Leith Street just down the hill a block away from the Playhouse.

On 11 December 1953 the main streets of Leith Walk were brightly lit, with Christmas shopping well underway. Busy crowds stared into shop windows unaware of the grim tragedy that had taken place just a short distance away. At no. 5 Marshall's Court the alarm had been given.

Two little girls had gone out to play together at 3 p.m. Told to come home before dark, it was now 5 p.m. and there was no sign of them. Lesley Sinclair was four and a half, her friend Margaret Johnston just three years old.

Margaret's father left their home at 9 Queen's Place and set off in search of the two children. He went first to her aunt Mrs Watt's house where Margaret was a frequent visitor. Learning that neither of the children had been there, he panicked and the police were notified. A neighbourhood search was organised. Someone had noticed the girls had been playing near one of the buildings. One man in the party thought he heard a child's cry and jumped over a wooden barrier to investigate. He found nothing, but the spot was directly opposite the entrance of no. 5 and the cries that he heard were possibly from the second-floor flat. The children had been missing for several hours and it was now fully dark.

Searchers armed with torches had spread out from the huddle of tenements and the maze of courts and alleys as far afield as Calton Hill overlooking Greenside Row, the area where both girls lived. Defeated after a futile search of every bush and derelict building, they returned to continue the hunt nearer home, only eighty yards away from the busy and brilliantly lit thoroughfare of Leith Street. While the search had been proceeding, Christmas shoppers and groups of young people returning from dances remained unaware of the concentrated police activity in the adjoining streets.

The bodies of Lesley and Margaret were eventually found in a lavatory in the tenement at 5 Marshall's Court where Lesley lived. They had been savagely beaten about the head and face.

The alarm had been raised after several tenants on the second floor had been unable to get into the shared lavatory. At last a woman forced the door open and her screams brought the other neighbours running to the grim scene.

Margaret was carried into the house of her grandmother Margaret Curran and, as news of the tragedy spread in the early hours of the morning, groups of men and women gathered at street corners and outside houses in the vicinity of Marshall's Court. Many had risen from their beds and hastily dressed. All were deeply shocked by the murder of two little girls who they had known so well.

In the ill-lit court which formed the square, entered from a side street, police cars with flashing lights were massed and groups of uniformed police officers stationed around the entrance to no. 5. At last they led out a small grey-haired Irishman wearing a sports jacket and collarless shirt. His name was John Lynch, aged forty-five and a resident in the same block of the tenement as Lesley.

At the trial before the High Court on 24 March 1954, Lynch was accused of sexually assaulting Lesley in his house at 5 Marshall's

Court or in a common lavatory on the stair. He had then com-pressed her nose and mouth and tied a ligature around her neck. It was understood that Lesley was still conscious when she was found but died shortly afterwards. Lynch murdered Margaret by either tying a necktie, a piece of stocking or part of an apron round her neck. Lesley was an only child. The parents of Margaret had a two-year-old son.

The first witness was Lesley's mother, who was distraught. She described Lesley as a healthy little girl, bright and intelligent, who had left the house with her chum Margaret at 3 p.m. When they hadn't returned by 3.45 p.m., she set off in search of them with Margaret's mother. At 5 p.m. the frantic mothers notified the police.

Mrs Sinclair had arranged to meet her husband on Leith Walk at 5.30 p.m. on his way home from his work as a blacksmith. She looked into Moir's Bar beside the old Theatre Royal and saw her husband standing beside Lynch. She called to him and both men came over.

When she told her husband of her fears and the neighbours' fruitless search for the two little girls, Lynch told her to calm down and said consolingly, 'You seem a bit worried. I'll buy you a drink to keep your courage up.' She accepted.

Afterwards, walking back towards the house, Lynch told her he had spoken to the little girls earlier that afternoon. 'They called the Dubliner "Uncle Paddy",' she said, and when she went into Margaret's grandmother's house, Lynch went with her.

By now everyone was distraught. The girls' mothers were hys-terical and Lynch said if anyone 'had done in the children' and he could find them, he would kill them.

At about 11 p.m. Mrs Sinclair heard someone shouting that the children had been found. She went up to the landing and some-one handed Lesley into her arms. As her husband took the child from her, she collapsed.

John Sinclair told the court that he used to have a drink with

Lynch now and then in Moir's Bar and was shocked when he saw him escorted from the house in police custody. Lynch had turned to him and said, 'They are trying to pin it on me.'

Mrs Curran said that her granddaughter had come to the house with Lesley. She had given them both a 'piece' before they had rushed off to play and they had been seen by the street orderly at 3 p.m. that afternoon playing on the steps at the back of the Salon Picture House.

Mrs McKail, occupant of the top flat of no. 5, said that her door was opposite Lynch's. While she was having tea with her family at about 5 p.m. that day, she had heard Lynch out on the landing, talking to somebody or talking to himself. She was accustomed to his language and she had heard the lavatory door being banged violently.

Someone had also banged against her door and she had shouted, 'In the name of God, what is that?', but hadn't investigated further as she was in a hurry. They were all going to the pictures. On the way out she had wanted to go to the lavatory but couldn't get in as the snib had fallen down.

They got back at 9.45 p.m. when the young people went to join the searchers for the missing children, leaving McKail and her daughter in the house. When the search party returned at nearly 11 p.m., her neice Elizabeth wanted to go to the lavatory but returned saying that the door was locked.

McKail said, 'You know how to open it, take the knife.' They forced the door open and Elizabeth saw something lying on the floor. She ran back into the house and shouted, 'There's someone in the toilet.' McKail went to investigate.

The missing children were lying on the floor behind the door. She shouted, 'We've found them! We've found them!', and Lynch came out on to the landing and asked what had happened. When she told him, he made no comment.

Later, when the police were taking a statement from McKail's family, Lynch again appeared on the landing and asked what all this nonsense was taking names and addresses. He was talking loudly and saying that if he could get his hands on the people who had harmed the little girls he would strangle them. He pushed forward several times and interrupted the police, asking when they were going to see him. The detective in charge of the investigation thought that he might be drunk since Lynch seemed very excited and kept saying, 'Take my name. I'll tell you how it was done.' When at last they went to his door at 2.13 a.m. Lynch let them in.

He pulled on his trousers and went to sit down on a chair where the detective saw a piece of apron cloth which he was sure was the identical pattern to the piece around Lesley's neck. It was torn at the shoulder strap.

Lynch watched the police looking round and shouted to a woman who was in the bed, 'There is something coming up here, Annie. Get up quick.' The detective observed that low down on the left sleeve of Lynch's shirt there was a small stain that might be blood.

At Lynch's trial on 24 March 1954 the public benches at the High Court were crowded to capacity. People lined the kerb of the north side of Parliament Square in the hope of getting a glimpse of his arrival from Saughton Prison. Nearly fifty witnesses were cited by the Crown and the jury included six women. The trial was expected to last for several days, with forty-nine productions listed for the Crown including three joint forensic medical reports, a book of thirty-three photos, articles of clothing and a sample of hair.

Mrs Annie Hall (forty-two), a kitchenmaid and Lynch's common law wife, was the first witness. She had lived with Lynch in Marshall's Court for twelve years and on the morning of 11 December had left him in bed as he was not working. That night they both went to bed early. Later she heard him shouting, something about finding a girl. Lynch got out of bed but did not leave the house until the detective came to the door when he shouted, 'Take me. I did it.'

The evidence showed that Lesley, found with her dress over her head, had been sexually assaulted before being suffocated. 'Horse hair' of the kind used for stuffing mattresses was found on both children's clothing – on the back of Lesley and front of Margaret. There was also horse hair on Lynch's clothing and hairs from both girls' heads.

The children were killed sometime between 3.10 p.m. when they were last seen and 5 p.m. They had been in Lynch's house and he had killed them there and put their bodies in the lavatory after 5 p.m. The times were precise as the lavatory had been used by the tenants before then, its door generally being left unlocked unless it was occupied.

The verdict of 'guilty' was unanimous. The sentence of 'death by hanging' was carried out at Saughton Prison on 23 April 1954.

But what sort of things were going on in 5 Marshall's Court at that time? One of the neighbours, Margaret's stepfather John Curran, said that before the date of the murder his mother had complained about strange men going up to both Lynch's house and to the McKails' next door at about midnight.

And what about Lynch and Annie? Did she not suspect anything? It seems horrendous that after killing two small girls Lynch could calmly go to bed early with her.

And what had driven him to invite the two little girls into his flat and kill them? They knew and trusted 'Uncle Paddy' as a neighbour and a friend of their parents – the sort of person those same parents would have had no qualms about leaving their children with. Was he a paedophile? Was there some secret story of regular child abuse with these two small girls which ended on that particular day in violence and death?

5 Marshall's Court has ceased to exist. There is now only one house left, no. 3 – the murder house being pulled down and replaced by a railed-off private car park for the impersonal business premises which dominate the area. But the ghost of what was once a busy tenement area still remains behind no. 3, an old set of

stone steps leading up to a drying green, once the centre of the court and a safe playground for small children.

1953 saw the coronation of Elizabeth the Second of England and the First of Scotland, as patriots were eager to point out! There was a rash of street parties. The Edinburgh Military Tattoo was fifty years old, an outstanding success since its first annual performance on the Castle Esplanade, and with the Second World War now almost a distant memory, Edinburgh Council were turning their attention to condemned housing in the city.

People were still living in houses that were little more than insanitary hovels. The idea of a shared lavatory belongs to a bygone age, but in the '50s there was such a desperate shortage of housing that families moved into former Army service huts, living in near squalour.

So began the Council's attempt to tackle the massive post-War housing problem. The bulldozers moved in to clear the slums and derelict buildings, while the Council rehoused the residents as it began its major house-building programme.

The grim streets of the Pleasance tenements – with their shared landings, shared lavatories and broken windows – vanished. That was the good side of the housing programme which also saw the destruction of many fine Georgian houses.

Among the deeply mourned casualties were the historic St James Square and George Square, which today would have been refurbished and have had conservation notices slapped on them. Instead, they vanished under soulless tower blocks where the old community street life of working-class Edinburgh was lost forever.

75 BROUGHTON STREET, 1987

Map ref. 16

Cross Leith Walk from Marshall's Court to a stairwell in Broughton Street where the body of a man was found on 7 May 1987. He had been brutally murdered, battered over the head with a blunt instrument.

Alan Borwick was a loner, well known to local publicans and shopkeepers in Dublin Street where he lived in one room. All that was known about him was that he was divorced, unemployed and, although quiet and polite when sober, was to be avoided as argumentative and abusive when drunk.

On the night of his death he was seen at 8.30 p.m. in the Barony Bar reeling toward Broughton Street very drunk. At 9 p.m. he was at the Phoenix Bar and a few minutes later was seen heading back towards the Barony Bar again. His next sighting was at the Deep Sea carryout, Antigua Street, where he bought a meal.

Just after 10 p.m. he was in Forth Street, playing a mouth organ and shouting and swearing at a teenager with fair or ginger hair wearing a green sweatshirt. Fifteen minutes later the two were at the corner of Forth and Broughton Street, still arguing. According to one passerby, it seemed that Borwick was demanding something from the youth.

'They seemed to be having a normal conversation at this stage, as if Mr Borwick was trying to tap the lad for a cigarette.' Half an hour later they were seen walking towards the Loon Moon Chinese restaurant close to where Borwick lived. This was the last time he was seen alive.

A few minutes later the youth was spotted alone outside the Peter Dominic off-licence on the opposite side of the road from the restaurant. Between 9 and 10 p.m. he had possibly been a customer in Crombies Bar in Broughton Street. At 10.50 p.m. neighbours and passers-by remembered hearing shouting coming from the tenement stair where Borwick's body was found.

A warm summer night, there were a lot of people about, walking or standing drinking at the open doors of various public houses. Despite pleas for information from the public, the only clue that the police had, was the chance meeting between Borwick and the teenager, to whom he took exception and got involved in a drunken argument. A neighbour at no. 95 who was on friendly terms with Borwick saw him with the teenager near the chip shop and heard him shout something about a lighter – 'Hand me back my lighter' – as if he was demanding it back. He confirmed that Borwick usually got 'steaming drunk' on receiving his unemployment benefit.

Did Borwick's other neighbours know more than they were telling? Was he in one of those moods where he'd be ready to pick a fight with anyone passing by? And had he learned too late this time that he had chosen a tough young adversary with fatal consequences? Nine months later the police were still appealing for evidence, the murder unsolved, but with one suspect who fitted the description. John Vetch, aged seventeen, already had a police record, having been convicted of sixteen offences since September 1986, and he had been seen in the area on the night of Borwick's killing. Taken into custody yet again in March 1988, this time on housebreaking charges, he made a statement about Borwick's death, claiming it was an accident, that he did not mean it to happen.

Charged with Borwick's murder, Vetch lodged a special plea of self-defence and claimed that on the night of 7 May he was at the dog racing at Powderhall Stadium. He admitted to being in the area and stopping on the way home to buy a fish supper. As he was walking past a door on Broughton Street, he picked up a cigarette lighter dropped by Borwick, who was drunk and knocked the bag of chips out of his hand.

Vetch maintained that Borwick had then grabbed him by the arm, pulled him into a stairway and begun to hit him, knocking him to the floor. He got up and grabbed the man by the neck. There was a fight and Borwick threw a stone at him which Vetch threw back. It hit Borwick on the head. Vetch said he later told friends about it in a pub.

The police pathologist said that Borwick 'drowned' in his own blood after being severely beaten about the head. He also had seven broken ribs, cuts and bruises, and had drunk either fifteen pints of beer or eight double whiskies.

The jury at Vetch's trial returned a majority verdict of culpable homicide, plus a charge of robbery for stealing the dead man's watch. He was sent to a young offenders' institution for twelve years.

Borwick was a sad case, a man who had fallen on hard times and who could be abusive with humans but, according to his neighbour at no. 95, cared for small animals like guinea pigs. Perhaps the Boys Brigade badge still proudly worn in his lapel was a memento of some happy period in his youth.

Why did it take the police ten months to make an arrest? The silence of the numerous people who must have seen the two together is not surprising if Borwick's violent behaviour made him a less than popular resident. And regulars in the local pub who had seen the two men together were perhaps well aware of the young man's identity but had their own reasons for not revealing it. But why did the neighbour eventually decide to come forward after Vetch had been arrested? And why did Vetch confess to murder if the eyewitness had only seen the two arguing over a lighter?

CALTON HILL, 1913

Map ref. 17

Heading up towards Princes Street brings you close to Calton Hill, the site of the ancient jail which in 1913 saw Edinburgh's first execution in the twentieth century. The proud boast was that this was the first for fifteen years.

The sensational case had shocked Edinburgh citizens. Patrick Higgins was a thirty-eight-year-old widower with previous convictions for child neglect. 'Of the labouring class,' the press wrote, 'Higgins slept out at night and cooked his food in his working shovel.' He had been found guilty of murdering his two sons, aged four and seven, by throwing them into a disused quarry at Niddry Mains Farm sometime between 25 October 1911 and 1 January 1912. There they had lain undiscovered until 8 June 1913, when their bodies were found floating in the water.

Condemned to death during a two-day trial on 10–11 August 1913, the sentence was carried out on 2 October. It was a perfect morning, according to the newspapers, and a crowd of some 500 men, women and children gathered on Calton Hill overlooking the jail. Their patient waiting was enlivened with entertainment by a street fiddler, whose repertoire included the melancholy but appropriate rendering of 'Lost Chord'.

Inside the jail, where some of the warders were dealing with their first hanging, the atmosphere was tense. Due to the lack of experienced staff, the press would be excluded from the execution chamber.

Resigned to his fate, Higgins offered no resistance on coming on to the death platform. The scaffold was over a well and the rope attached to an overhead beam. A warder appeared on top of the prison's eastern tower, attached the black flag to the rope . . . and waited.

When he hoisted the flag to half-mast at 8.03 a.m., Higgins had gone to his doom. But what had driven Higgins to this monstrous deed? What was his background? What had happened to his wife? How did she die? Press reports from the time are scant, but was Higgins a forerunner to a more enlightened age in which people take shotguns to their entire families and wipe out school children in playgrounds? And would Higgins now be regarded as criminally insane, driven by a breakdown of reason to destroy his own children?

A Note on Executioners

Higgins' executioner was John Ellis of Rochdale. When he applied to the Home Office for the post, his father 'played hell all round and cut him off without a farthing'. However, after a week's instruction at Newgate Prison in 1901, Ellis became an assistant to the Billingtons of Bolton, Lancashire, for whom executions were a family business.

James Billington's predecessor, James Berry, had executed three Scottish murderers by hanging. A former Bradford policeman, his application to the magistrates of Edinburgh was accepted in March 1884. His Scottish executions included Jessie King, the notorious Stockbridge baby-farmer who accepted unwanted children for a fee and then murdered them. After her hanging on 11 March 1889, Berry said '[Executing women] always made me shiver like a leaf.' It was his opinion that King would be the last woman hanged.

101

When Berry retired in 1892, James Billington became senior executioner and executed Scottish murderers between 1897 and 1898. With 147 executions to his credit over a twenty-seven-year career, he died in December 1901.

At that time the Home Office list of approved executioners also included Billington's two sons, Thomas and William, of whom William became the preferred successor. In November 1902 he executed Patrick Leggett in Glasgow and in July 1904 returned to execute Thomas Gunning, assisted by his brother. But in 1905 he went to jail himself for one month with hard labour for failing to maintain his estranged wife and their two children.

Such was the inheritance of John Ellis, who first came to Scotland in August 1908 to hang Edward Johnstone at Perth. His last execution was of Edith Thomson at Holloway Prison on 8 January 1923, and his long career ended following a breakdown in early October which lost him the opportunity of adding Edinburgh murderer Philip Murray (*see* pp. 80 –4) to his score of 202 executions in twenty-three-years – a list which included some of Britain's most infamous killers: Dr Hawley Harvey Crippen, George Joseph Smith and the Irish patriot Sir Roger Casement.

Ellis had already appeared before the magistrates for attempted suicide in 1924. But on Tuesday, 20 September 1932, having returned home drunk, he was sitting at the dining table with his family when he rushed to the kitchen, coming back with a razor and threatening to kill his wife and cut off his daughter's head. They both fled from the house, and his son arrived in time to see him sink to the floor with two severe lacerations to his throat.

When the police arrived, Ellis was lying dead in a pool of blood. Considering the violence of his trade and the nightmares it must have induced, this seemed not an inappropriate end.

THE ROYAL BRITISH HOTEL, PRINCES STREET, 1971

Death by Fire

Map ref. 18

Princes Street, the elegant thoroughfare at the heart of Edinburgh's busy city centre, has seen its fair share of crime over the past hundred years. Mayhem and murder, from petty thefts to late-night assaults and muggings, and individuals with a score to settle, have all ended in sentences of culpable homicide.

An impressive murder setting is the old established Victorian hotel on the well-illuminated stretch of Princes Street opposite Waverley Railway Station. The opulence and calm of the Royal British Hotel was shattered when arson turned to homicide thirty years ago.

In May 1971 Robert Docherty was sent to work at the hotel because of a shortage of staff. The young man unfortunately had a leaning towards arson, a somewhat precarious preoccupation for anyone who was to be employed as chef in the hotel kitchen.

Two mysterious fires had broken out in one week when a cleaner had found 'something smouldering on the back stairs' and was under the impression that it was a waste-paper basket. These incidents alone were not enough to arouse suspicions that an arsonist was at work. Accidental fires are dismissed as unfortunate but inevitable in any busy hotel where late-night revellers or guests smoking in bedrooms are careless with cigarettes.

Early on Sunday morning, 30 May 1971, however, the manager was awakened by the night porter and told that there was a serious fire in the hotel. Guests were being led to safety from their bedrooms and the manager saw thick black smoke coming from a bedroom which was under reconstruction.

'At first I couldn't get down the fire escape because of the smoke,' he said. 'Then it thinned a little bit and I just ran down as fast as I could. I was the last person out of the hotel.'

Or so he thought. But not everyone had escaped. A forty-nine-year-old woman from Glasgow had been trapped by the blaze and overcome by fumes. When at last the fire was brought under control, her charred body was found lying near some stairs on the third floor.

The detective in charge of the fatal accident inquiry interviewed a number of the staff, including the chef Docherty, who said that he had first heard of the outbreak from the head porter. He said that he had tried to fight the blaze but, when he realised it was hopeless, had set off the fire alarm and wakened the staff and guests.

The detective's suspicions were aroused on learning of the two earlier fires that week. Three days later members of the staff were again interviewed on the instructions of DCI James Campbell.

A check on the latest members of staff and the two fires since Docherty's arrival marked him down as the prime suspect. Meanwhile, he had been transferred to a hotel in North Berwick and when interviewed there by the police made another statement.

When certain points did not square up to his earlier version of events taken at the scene of the Royal British Hotel fire, Docherty was cautioned, taken to the police station in North Berwick and thence to Edinburgh. Questioned on the discrepancies in his statements, Docherty said, 'You've found out.'

He confessed that he had started a fire in the Edinburgh hotel by throwing a lighted cigarette into a box of rubbish. But he denied that he had wilfully placed an inflammable liquid in either the unfurnished room on the second floor or in the corridor. Nor had he set fire to a cardboard box containing waste paper on a staircase so that a female guest trying to escape had been overcome by fumes and died. He also denied maliciously starting the two earlier fires in the hotel by setting fire to a quantity of waste paper.

'The Sunday fire wasn't meant. I went into the room where the paper was, then I came out and went into the other room. There was a smell of Evostick and a box with a lot of rubbish in it. I was smoking a cigarette. I just threw the cigarette away into the box. The box just gave a puff and burst into flames. I never panicked. I just looked for a fire extinguisher but I couldn't find one. So I just went back to the kitchen and stayed there.'

The assistant firemaster stated that when he arrived at the hotel about 7.45 a.m., he had seen a large column of flames coming from a room on the upper floor where people were being rescued by the escape apparatus. The woman from Glasgow was not so fortunate.

In his evidence at the High Court trial of Docherty, the firemaster said that he had ruled out accidental fire: 'The pattern of the fire was not natural. It suggests some form of pre-treatment.' He thought that inflammable liquid or material must have been introduced to the second-floor room and sprinkled along part of the corridor leading away from it and possibly up a flight of stairs.

There appeared to have been two flash-points – one in the bedroom and one further along the corridor sending a ball of fire like a napalm bomb along and up the stairs.

'I could not relate the fierceness of a fairly severe fire to the materials in the room,' he said. 'Experiments using waste-paper buckets showed it was very difficult to start a fire as quick as the one in which the woman died. It could take about eighty minutes to start a fire with a lighted cigarette.' In his opinion the fire was deliberate. It was not the result of Docherty throwing a cigarette end into a rubbish bin.

'I never expected anything like this,' said Docherty. 'I am sorry. The whole thing was stupid – the woman that died will be on my mind for the rest of my days.'

The jury was unimpressed and took forty-five minutes to reach a unanimous verdict. The twenty-five-year-old chef, who was married with one child, was found guilty of wilful fire-raising. But he was acquitted of the charge of culpable homicide, which alleged that he had deliberately used inflammable liquid to encourage the blaze.

Docherty was sentenced to nine years' imprisonment. His crime, the Lord Justice-Clerk added, was 'a reckless, wicked and wilful act'.

Released on bail six months later in December, Docherty appeared at Glasgow Sheriff Court pleading guilty to charges of fraud. He was sentenced to eighteen months' imprisonment. The nine-year sentence would then follow its expiry.

THE ROYAL BRITISH HOTEL, PRINCES STREET, 1977

Child Murder

Map ref. 18

On 4 October 1977, five years after the fire in the Royal British Hotel, an eight-year-old boy was found naked in a bed on the second floor. He was dead and the man who had accompanied the boy to the hotel a few days earlier posing as his father was to appear in connection with it.

A tragic case unfolded. Tommy Hayden had been missing for nearly three weeks from St Kiernan's Children's Home at Rathdrum in County Wicklow and the Irish police were now taking an intense interest in the case since the boy's distraught mother blamed Ireland's social welfare system for Tommy's death.

When Josey Hayden returned with her three young boys to Dublin from England following her husband's death, the children were put into Madonna House Children's Home at Blackrock. Their mother was allegedly ill-treating them and was no longer able to support them as the State had withdrawn her widow's pension. Under Irish law, this is only granted if the recipient is living alone, and Mrs Hayden had admitted that she was now sharing her flat with a 'protector' and was pregnant with twins. 'I was terrified of living in the block of flats alone,' she said, 'and when my friend came to live with me I felt safe for the first time.

Vandals did not attack my flat knowing there was a man around.'
Regardless of this, however, she had issued an appeal to the
children's home for the return of Tommy. The circumstances were
exceptional.

John Dwyer, a twenty-five-year-old house father at the children's home, had gone missing at the same time as Tommy who,
it was said, 'he had treated like a son'. Their tragic flight had
ended in the Royal British Hotel where, in the bathroom of room
117, Dwyer had assaulted the boy and held his head under the
bath water where he drowned. Dwyer had then tried to commit
suicide and told the police that Tommy was better off dead than
going back to the home where he was unhappy. He added, 'It is
just a pity that it didn't work for me.'

According to reports from the children's home, Dwyer's work
was excellent and 'he was most attentive to his duties'. He had
first met Tommy and his two brothers in 1974 in Madonna House,
Blackrock outside Dublin, where he then worked and where the
boys had been placed because of the alleged neglect by their
mother. Three years later Tommy was moved to St Kiernan's in
County Wicklow, but he was unhappy and at least once had run
back to Dwyer at Blackrock.

On learning of Mrs Hayden's request for Tommy's return,
Dwyer – faced with a desperate emotional situation – sold his car
for £1000 and flew with the boy to London, where he booked in at
a Heathrow hotel as father and son. In September they travelled
to Edinburgh and, after trying two hotels but failing to obtain a
room with an en suite bathroom, they were eventually successful
with the Princes Street hotel.

Last seen at dinner on the night before the tragedy, one of the
porters observed a 'Do Not Disturb' notice on the door of room
117. On the following morning Dwyer went to the deputy
manager and told him that his son had died.

Hotel staff went to the room where Tommy's body was lying on
the bed. The hotel doctor examined him and discovered blister

marks. Dwyer said his illegitimate son had drowned accidentally while they had been indulging in horseplay. He had then tried to commit suicide by taking an overdose of drugs.

Interviewed by DCI Brian Cunningham, Dwyer said, 'Tommy became very dependent on me. He threatened other members of the staff he would tell me if they punished him for anything. He ran away from the home and was gone for three days. He was later transferred and told me he was unhappy and was going to run away. He asked if he could come with me when I was leaving. I sold my car and bought plane tickets for London. I kept thinking it would be in the papers about me taking Tommy away. I was looking for a flat but I couldn't see a flat coming and the money was getting low so I decided it would be best to kill Tommy and myself.'

Dwyer was tried at the High Court and jailed for life for Tommy's murder.

Reading between the lines, this was a very tragic situation and in some ways reminiscent of Bernard MacLaverty's novel and the film *Lamb*. Was twenty-five-year-old Dwyer a paedophile? Or was he obsessed by the unfortunate circumstances of Tommy and his two brothers? – abnormal behaviour in a house father who might be expected to be able to deal with such situations and to have learned to distance himself emotionally from his frequently distressed and unhappy charges. A whiff of child abuse hangs in the air, as does the smell of bureaucracy which could well, as the boy's mother claimed, have initiated this whole tragedy in the first place.

THE OLD TOWN

THE WORLD'S END PUB, NETHERBOW, 1977

Map ref. 19

It is just a short distance from Princes Street, up the Mound and down the historic Royal Mile, to The World's End pub. Situated at the Netherbow Port, once the main exit south of the city, in medieval times this area beyond the Flodden Wall was regarded as the end of Edinburgh. In the twentieth century it became the site of one of Edinburgh's most baffling murders.

On a busy Saturday night, 15 October 1977, two seventeen-year-old girls, Helen Scott and Christine Eadie – close friends who had met in their first year at Firrhill High School – were on a pub crawl with two other mates. After visiting various pubs, they finally arrived at The World's End.

High on Edinburgh's 'Saturday night out' list, it was very popular and crowded with customers – well over 200 in number. According to people who were drinking there that night, the jukebox was playing the latest chart-toppers: 'You Light up my Life' and 'Nobody does it better'. Older folk talked of Bing Crosby's death, aged seventy-three, after collapsing on a Madrid golf course. On the home front, Prime Minister Jim Callahan battled with inflation.

The two girls – Christine from Colinton Mains Green and Helen from Comiston – had taken a seat opposite the front door. They were approached by two men. The first, who spoke primarily to

Helen, was between 27 and 30 years of age, 5'5" tall, of average build, with short wavy dark hair parted on the side, a pale complexion, clean shaven and wearing loose dark pin-stripe trousers. The trousers were very distinctive 'high-waister bags' not worn by a 'mod' dresser. They had two pocket flaps at the front and rear, with four or five buttons running vertically above the zip fly. The man was also wearing a brown jumper and light coloured shirt.

The second man was the same height and build, with short wavy hair, a fresh complexion and may have had a moustache, wearing a blue/grey jumper and black trousers.

The girls' mates left them to head off to a party, but Helen and Christine decided to stay and talk to the two men, who had local accents and were pushy and insistent. Although the girls seemed to be keeping them at arms' length, they were obviously enjoying the attention, being chatted up and bought drinks. One of them was laughing, saying to the men. 'You're only interested in sex.'

There were few sightings of the four of them after that.

Who was to notice the departure of two young girls and two older men in such a crowded setting? One of the more definite sightings that emerged later came from a couple walking up the High Street from Holyrood Park towards The World's End. They saw two girls in the company of two men and one of the girls appeared to be under the influence of drink. She slipped out of her shoe and shouted out to the other girl, calling her 'Chris'.

That was the last known sighting. The girls failed to appear at their homes that night and next day the alarm was raised.

But it was already too late for Helen and Christine.

That morning their naked bodies were discovered dumped a few miles apart in East Lothian: first Christine on the foreshore at Gosford Bay, near Longniddry; then Helen off the Huntingdon to Coates Road near Haddington. They had both been beaten, raped and strangled. No serious attempt had been made to hide the bodies.

114

The murder squad went into immediate action. It was obvious that the girls had been offered a lift when they left The World's End and the police wanted to trace a dark Ford transit-type van which had been parked outside the pub between 11 and 11.15 p.m.

Fifteen minutes after Christine and Helen had been seen walking down St Mary's Street, a dark blue Wolseley was seen, driven from Holyrood Park into London Road and Willowbrae. The driver had a moustache and there were four or five occupants. The police also wanted to interview anyone who had been in the Allan Ramsay Tavern in the High Street that evening at about 9 p.m. as two men answering their descriptions were seen in the upstairs bar at that time.

On the same night, at 11.50 p.m., a man aged 30–33 with mousey brown collar-length hair and a Mexican-type moustache made a phone call from a kiosk in Drem, East Lothian. A very agitated man, who kept the kiosk door open with his left foot; a man who was one of the occupants of a dark van parked nearby and who was later seen driving off in the direction of Edinburgh. A Ford Cortina Mark 3 was seen to drive into the No. 1 car park on the Port Seton to Aberlady road that night.

Police at Leith also received a phone call from a man who said he was in Selkirk. He claimed to have vital information but as he was an under-age drinker he was scared of the consequences. The police arranged a meeting, but he failed to turn up. Was this mystery caller the same 'Billy' who, in 1997 – twenty years later – claimed that he had known the girls' killers?

The murders had been carried out in cold blood and, according to police psychologists, the killer was most likely a psychopath helped by a friend. He had been clinically methodical and had probably shown no outward sign of anxiety to his friends, family or workmates. It was also possible that his partner in crime was a very frightened man who had changed his appearance and lifestyle since the murder and the police wanted to hear from anyone who had noticed such a sudden change in a relative, friend or neighbour.

They were also investigating a possible link between the World's End murders and those of Mathilda Miller, aged thirty-six, and Agnes Cooney, aged twenty-three, since the similarities were striking. Two weeks before Christine and Helen were killed, the body of Mathilda Miller was discovered in a lovers' lane at Langbank off the M8. She had been strangled. On 8 December, Agnes Cooney was found strangled near Caldercruix.

Detectives believed that the two men who murdered the Edinburgh girls may have assaulted other women as well and that someone was withholding information. If the killers were not caught, there was a good chance that they would claim other victims.

A reward of £1500 was offered, collected from staff of Helen's employers at Kiltmakers, who had two Princes Street shops; from sales staff at Scottish Telecom Board where Helen's father Morain Scott worked; and from Christine's employer, J. N. Underwood, surveyors.

Locally, both Tynecastle and Easter Road football grounds made announcements about the reward as did local cinemas. The investigating team believed – and still believe – that some-one was shielding the killers because of misplaced loyalty or fear of reprisals. They promised police protection for anyone who had vital information and who was scared to come forward.

The police were making exhaustive inquiries but a year later they were still baffled. A seven-foot high filing cabinet at Dalkeith police station was crammed with fifty files containing statements and forms from 15,000 people interviewed by the police, the Army and Interpol. They were also anxious to hear from any woman who had been sexually assaulted during the twelve months since the murders but who had not yet reported the attack. But the trail had long gone cold.

Twenty-five years later the inquiry is still in progress for what became Scotland's biggest unsolved murders and now over 20,000 people have been interviewed.

In December 1997 there was an interesting development. A man who wished to remain anonymous and was called 'Billy' by the police claimed to know those who were responsible for the girls' murders. He gave the names of two men. The evidence came at a crucial time for the police, who had just announced that they had formed a small unit of detectives in an effort to trace the killers. They were immediately on the case. Was this the lead they were looking for?

'Billy' said he had given two men a lift to Edinburgh after picking them up on a quiet road near Aberlady, East Lothian, hours after the killings in 1977. The spot was close to where the body of Christine was found. The body of her friend Helen was found just three miles away.

'Billy' said he was a former car thief and that he was returning to Edinburgh in a stolen Cortina when he gave the two men a lift. He urged the police to re-examine the evidence, claiming that one of the men had since been murdered and the other had been convicted of rape.

'Billy' said he recognised one of the men as a friend of his older brother and initially assumed they had been breaking into a house. He did not immediately inform the police as he quickly guessed why the pair may have been at the side of the road and just as quickly guessed what could happen to him if he informed on them.

'At the time I was a young guy and this gave me quite a fright, knowing what could happen to me. They were pretty well known. They were pretty hard guys.' The men had tracked him down again only days after the murders and warned him to keep his mouth shut. They didn't need to say what about.

'Billy' described the clothing worn by the pair in detail and exactly where he had picked them up, but could not explain how the pair got to East Lothian or what happened to the vehicle they must have used.

He added, 'Other people know about this. Other females have been bothered by them over the years. I was terrified of those two and I was just seventeen when it happened so I didn't tell anyone. In 1994 I did tell detectives and now I want to see justice done. But they still have family around Edinburgh and I need protection from them.'

'Billy' said he wouldn't give evidence out of fear of the men's families. He added, 'I want to go to court. This has been on my conscience. But I want protection from the police.'

The two men he named had been questioned by detectives in 1977 but later released. One of them had indeed been later murdered and the other man was released from prison a few years ago after serving several years for a series of rapes. He is now believed to be living as a businessman in London.

The men 'Billy' named may have had an innocent reason for being in East Lothian, or a not-so-innocent one unconnected with the murders. His account was perhaps not enough for the police to work on, but detectives started to re-examine every scrap of information and in 1997 the latest in computer and DNA technology was made available to them. The first full DNA profile was obtained from samples, and the same genetic profile was obtained from both crime scenes.

Between October 1998 and April 1999 the police swabbed around 500 men, most of whom had been suggested in the past but could not be finally eliminated. Many, who had lived under the cloud of suspicion with family members for a long time, had been very willing to co-operate. However, after carrying out the swab tests, a lot of possible suspects were cleared.

The long saga of the World's End murder investigations had by then taken some remarkable twists. Peter Sutcliffe, The Yorkshire Ripper, was quizzed by the police but rejected as a possible suspect. Inquiries were made as far away as Plymouth after it was suggested that fishermen could have been responsible. An Army angle was also investigated when it was thought that soldiers could have been involved, and later oil workers from the rigs were among the 20,000 people questioned.

In 2001 the case was featured on the television series *Britain's Most Wanted*. As a result, 125 phone calls were received from the public, mainly naming people they suspected could be involved with the murders because of either a change in behaviour at the time of the killings or some other suspicious pattern. The police then interviewed seventy men and obtained mouth swabs for DNA testing.

In January 2001 the National Crime Faculty team travelled up from England. They specialise in unsolved crimes and reviewed the case with local police for three days. They provided a behavioural profiler, forensic scientists and geographic profiles, and suggested that the deposition sites for the girls hinted at local knowledge of East Lothian. It could well have been people who lived there, were born and brought up in the area or had worked there. They suggested testing items such as clothing and bindings using new DNA techniques which allow the examination of items down to the size of a skin cell.

The National Crime Faculty visit was followed up by officers taking swabs from men in East Lothian and other parts of the UK for a couple of months. The police also contacted their counterparts in other countries with national databases so that they could check their systems in an effort to secure a DNA match – in case the man or men have since emigrated.

For a while they were hopeful of a breakthrough when US naval intelligence officers believed they might have stumbled across possible links with the World's End murders. While investigating a killing in America, a former US serviceman based near Dunoon, under investigation for another crime, was suspected of being involved in the murders but DNA evidence ruled him out.

It is twenty-five years since the murders. Despite inquiries spread throughout the country and the latest forensic technology, the case remains unsolved but the police are still hopeful that one day justice will be done.

They only have DNA for one man but have always been convinced that two were involved – that one did it and the other was an accomplice.

There is also the chilling thought, as so often happens in unsolved crimes, that perhaps one of the girls' killers now has a family of his own – 'a businessman now living in London', as 'Billy' claimed.

ST JOHN'S HILL, 1945

Map ref. 20

Turn back the calendar half a century to an investigation involving one of Edinburgh's most famous detectives, Superintendent William Merrilees.

The victim was a child, eight-year-old Phyllis Merritt, found dead in an air-raid shelter between St John's Hill and Holyrood Road on 12 July 1945. The walls of the shelter were blood-stained and the girl was lying in a pool of blood with extensive head injuries.

Phyllis's mother lived in 6 St James Place. Her father was serving on an aircraft carrier in the Pacific, and she was their second child, with brothers aged ten and six. She had been spending a holiday with her grandmother, Mrs Rigg, at 8 St John's Hill. As she had been in the habit of going between her own home and that of her grandmother, no immediate alarm was felt over her absence, her mother presuming Phyllis was with Mrs Rigg and Mrs Rigg believing that Phyllis had returned to her own home.

Mrs Rigg said that Phyllis, a bright intelligent little girl, was a pupil at East London Street School. She had left her house on the Wednesday morning to visit an aunt at Brown Street and it was understood that she had later gone to play in Holyrood Park. She had returned to her aunt's house at noon and at about 1 p.m. left to return to St John's Hill. When she did not arrive, it was presumed that she had gone back to her own home.

Neighbours were extremely distressed as Phyllis, 'a very nice pleasant little girl', used to play with their own children when she came to stay with her grandmother. It was a great shock when policemen called and told them of the tragedy.

Phyllis had last been seen on the day of her murder having lunch in a nearby café with her seventeen-year-old uncle, Robert Carmichael Rigg of St John's Hill. On the afternoon of the following day, Rigg reported to a police inspector at CID that he had discovered the body of his niece in an air-raid shelter.

The area has long been transformed by the building of *The Scotsman* offices and the new Parliament. At the time the air-raid shelter was one of a number of brick-surface types just across from the tenement at St John's Hill. The door was open and, as the lights had recently been removed, it was necessary to run a cable from the nearby brewery to enable medical experts to get enough light for their examination.

The circumstances of Rigg's statement and his demeanour were suspicious and he was charged with Phyllis's murder. He appeared in a court packed almost to capacity. Tousled-haired, without collar or tie, he was helped slowly into the dock, where he stood in a dazed condition, his replies scarcely audible.

The charge against Rigg was that, on 11 July, in an air-raid shelter on St John's Hill, he assaulted Phyllis Merritt, seized her by the neck, pressed her throat and struck her head against the wall and a bench, dragged her to the ground, struck her again on the head and shoulder with stones and did murder her.

A special defence was intimated to the effect that at the time the crime was committed the accused was insane, or alternatively in such a state of mental weakness as to make him irresponsible for his actions and the consequences thereof.

Superintendent Merrilees stepped into the witness box and told how Rigg went with him to the police station after the little girl's body had been discovered. Rigg had said he was prepared to remain there 'day and night' to help them find the murderer.

According to Merrilees, after Rigg had made a long statement about his movements, he suddenly remarked that he 'would give Superintendent Merrilees something'.

The Superintendent said he was suspicious that Rigg's story would have a very important bearing on the case, so he cautioned him and told him anything he said might be used in evidence. Rigg was given the chance of having his parents or a lawyer present, but refused.

The Lord Justice-Clerk, however, refused to admit evidence by a police superintendent as to a statement said to have been made voluntarily to him by the accused and a verdict of not guilty was brought in against Rigg.

Mrs Merritt, the girl's mother, stood up in court and pleaded for a chance to go back into the witness box. She was told to sit down but continued to cry. Her plea denied, she was removed half-fainting from the courtroom.

As Rigg left, there was a rush on the part of the public to see him. Relatives who waited outside threw their arms around him and kissed him.

A Note on William Merrilees

William Merrilees was one of the most colourful characters in the history of the Edinburgh City Police, frequently demonstrating why he had been dubbed 'the pocket-sized detective with the battleship reputation'.

At 5' 6", he had been too short to be accepted for the police and he had also lost the fingers of his left hand in an accident at a rope factory. But he received a special dispensation to join the Edinburgh City Police in 1924 after acquiring a reputation for courage and daring in rescuing a number of people from the waters of Leith Harbour and collecting a number of Royal Humane Society certificates in the process.

As well as being a swimmer, he was a boxer and footballer in

his youth, playing for Hawthornvale when they won the East of
Scotland Cup. His prowess as a swimmer, his courage and deter-
mination had come to the attention of the then Lord Provost, Sir
Thomas Hutchison, who made a special application on his behalf
to the Secretary of State for Scotland. The pleas were noted and
William Merrilees was accepted.

'A man of many disguises', he used them to good effect. As a
sergeant, he played a prominent part in breaking the Kosmo Club
case, a nightclub where call-girl operations were being run.

During the Second World War he also arrested the only German
spies known to have landed in Scotland. The story, worthy of a TV
drama, began in the early hours of 30 September 1940 when a man
and woman entered the little railway station of Buckpool, near
Buckie in Banffshire, and asked for tickets to London. This early-
morning request for a London train when most would have asked
for Edinburgh or Glasgow – plus the fact that their clothing
appeared to be damp up to the knees and their shoes covered in
wet sand – aroused the suspicions of the porter that they had
come ashore by boat. The local constable was informed and in due
course word reached Merrilees in Edinburgh who, disguised as a
porter, went aboard the train at Waverley Station and made a
dramatic arrest of the two spys with their suitcase containing a
radio transmitter. The man was later hanged. The woman was
given the option of the same fate or of becoming a counter-agent
for the British. She chose the latter.

In another operation, Merrilees was dressed as a baby and
wheeled through an Edinburgh park in a pram to apprehend a
man who was molesting nursemaids. The attacker must have
been extremely surprised when the 'baby' leaped out and arrested
him! On yet another occasion, he wandered the streets of
Edinburgh dressed as a woman – a disguise he admitted to enjoying greatly – in order to apprehend and arrest a bag-snatcher.

Born in Leith of poor parents, Merrilees rose from the ranks and
was appointed Chief Constable of Lothians and Peebles Police in

1950, at the age of fifty-one. He campaigned long and vigorously for the return of capital punishment for crimes of violence. 'I cannot understand those who think we should be lenient with thugs who attack elderly people and often seriously injure them.'

He was invited to stay at his post for an extra five years after reaching retirement age, the only chief constable in Britain to whom this special dispensation was given.

The holder of the King's Police Medal and a Knight of the Order of St Lazarus, the work he did for charity was almost as prominent as his police work and latterly even more so – particularly for the elderly and children, when he bought the railway station at Dolphinton in the Borders for their benefit when on holiday.

In 1959 'Willy' Merrilees – champion of law and order, a member of more than fifty organisations and friend of the friendless – was the subject of *This is Your Life*.

In 1966 his autobiography, *The Short Arm of the Law*, was published by John Long. Twice married, with one son, he died in August 1994 aged eighty-five. His funeral was attended by all those who had known and loved him, and many others to whom his career was already one of Edinburgh's great legends.

57 TRON SQUARE, 1954

Map ref. 21

On 28 February 1954 – just two months after the Marshall's Court tragedy on 11 December 1953 when two small girls were murdered (*see* p. 89–95) – there was a brutal domestic murder in the area now known as Hunter Square at the back of Edinburgh's historic Royal Mile.

In the early hours of the morning Mrs Elizabeth McGarry, aged thirty-nine, and her sixteen-year-old daughter and eighteen-year-old son from her first marriage, Jean and George Robertson were attacked in their home at 57 Tron Square. The mother had died in her home where her badly stabbed daughter was also found. The son had fled from the house. Bleeding, he had run along the balcony, down the twenty-four steps to the stone-paved quadrangle, and had sought sanctuary in the Hays' house at no. 42 where, finding the door locked, he had thrown himself through the kitchen window. There he had been murdered before his body was brought back to his home.

When Mr and Mrs Hay went to the police station at 3 a.m. they were almost hysterical. With the police officers, they went to no. 57 and saw heavy blood staining as well as naked footprints clearly visible on the concrete footway. They knocked on the door and received no answer but could hear somebody moving about inside so entering the house they saw McGarry's body clothed only in a brassiere and covered by a brown coat. Blood-stained clothing was strewn over the floor. Her dead son George was seated in an armchair. He had a puncture wound in the region of his heart, a gaping wound behind his left ear and a wound in his forearm. Jean came in through the bedroom door wearing an overcoat. She had wounds in her abdomen and arm. There was adhesive tape round her neck and her hands were tied together with flex.

Her father, George Alexander Robertson, was lying on the floor with his head inside the gas oven. He appeared to be unconscious and there was a fairly strong smell of gas, which was turned full on. He was removed from the oven and both he and Jean were taken away by ambulance.

The police found bloodstains which ran from the door of no. 57, along the corridor, down the stairs and out into the quadrangle. Beside these were the imprints of naked feet, which still remained in spite of the snow that had fallen. But none of the residents in the large block of tenement houses that made up one part of the Square were aware of the tragedy enacted below and above them while they were asleep. Only one neighbour, two flights above at no. 73, had heard a noise and had tried to arouse her husband. She had apparently heard the word, 'Help!' called several times but was afraid to investigate further.

The house where the bodies were found consisted of a room and a kitchen opening on to an outside railed gallery on the first floor of a four-storey tenement overlooking a large quadrangle. Surrounded on three sides by a high tenement, the lower part of what was once known as Tron Square looked out on the south side on to the Cowgate.

Shortly after the bodies had been found, the police issued a statement that, following an emergency call, they had found the dead woman and her son. Her seriously injured daughter had been removed by ambulance to the Royal Infirmary. The statement added, 'A man has been taken into custody in connection with the affair.'

Mr and Mrs Greig, McGarry's parents, also lived in Tron Square. Both were ill and the news was kept from Mrs Greig for twelve hours. A priest sat by her bedside when she was told.

Residents were shocked by the discovery of the bodies. Families stood at the doors in groups. All spoke highly of 'Lizzy' McGarry. One neighbour said that last summer she had been the leading spirit in organising the Square's Coronation celebration. The houses were gaily decorated and there was an outside party for the children in the quadrangle. The last relic of the occasion, a faded picture of the Queen, was still hanging over a window above no. 57 at the time of the murder.

The dead youth George, a coal porter, was a former pupil of St Patrick's R.C. School and had been awaiting the result of his medical examination for National Service. Jean, a former pupil at St Thomas's R.C. School, was employed by an Edinburgh paper-making firm. She had been in poor health for some time. The family had lived in the Craigmillar district before moving to Tron Square three years earlier. Mrs McGarry had lived in Tron Square before and the name plate on her front door was Greig, her maiden name.

George Alexander Robertson, aged forty, was arrested on a charge of murdering his former wife and son and also attempting to murder his daughter.

The charges to which he pleaded not guilty were:

1. That he had assulted Elizabeth Greig or Robertson or McGarry, tied her wrists with a piece of flex, bound her mouth with adhesive tape, and in the said house in Tron Square had repeatedly stabbed her with a knife – 'and did murder her'.
2. In the house occupied by Lawrence Hay, at 42 Tron Square, he assaulted George Alexander Robertson, junior, his son, and repeatedly stabbed him with a knife – 'and did murder him'.
3. In the house at 57 Tron Square he assaulted Jean Elizabeth Robertson, his daughter, tied her wrists with a piece of flex,

bound her mouth and legs with adhesive tape, and repeatedly stabbed her with a knife to her severe injury and to the danger of her life – 'and did attempt to murder her'.

The charges added that Robertson previously 'evinced malice and ill-will' towards his former wife and his son and daughter.

Forty-nine productions – including a sheath knife, a boning knife, a stick, a poker, a rolling-pin, medical reports and articles of clothing – were listed. Forty-one witnesses were called for the prosecution.

At Robertson's trial in June 1954 the first witness was his daughter Jean, who was given permission to remain seated while she gave evidence. Her mother was divorced from Robertson and had remarried, but her second husband had only lived with the family for a short time. Her father had returned and had been living in the house until shortly before 28 February when, after some trouble with his mother-in-law, he had left.

Asked if she was afraid of her father coming back, Jean replied yes and that they bolted the door and put a poker in the window, as well as a brush and chair behind the door.

She then described the night her mother and brother died. On returning home from a dance, she had found her mother in the house with several friends having a sing-song. Her brother had come home later. After the friends left, Jean said they had prepared to go to bed. She slept with her mother in one bed and her brother George in another in the same room.

'That night we forgot to put the chair behind the door.'

She had been awakened by the sound of her father whispering. After her mother had gone through to the kitchen, she wakened her brother. He had gone into the lobby and she had followed him.

Asked what happened next, Jean began to cry. 'I saw him sticking a knife in George's head.' Her brother had fallen to the floor and then her father had turned on her. He pushed her on to the bed and started stabbing her with a knife. She said she resisted as best she could and screamed.

She then heard the outside door being opened and her father running from the room and downstairs. He returned carrying her mother upstairs over his shoulder.

'I saw a big hole in her stomach. There was binding round her mouth, it might have been a handkerchief, and her hands were bound. My father brought her into the house and threw her down beside the cooker.'

Cross-examined, Jean denied that for some time her father had disapproved of her staying out late at night and that this had been the cause of trouble between them.

Mrs Catherine Hay, who had lived at 42 Tron Square at the time, said that on the fatal night she, her husband and two children had gone to bed. They were awakened by a noise, and she thought someone was fighting and had fallen against the door. The kitchen window was then broken and she heard young George shouting to her husband.

The boy came through the window and his father was behind with a knife in each hand. As the boy slumped to the floor, Mrs Hay said Robertson put the knife into him. When her husband tried to intervene, Robertson turned on him and said, 'Keep out of this or you'll get it too.' He then left but returned shortly afterwards and carried the boy away in his arms.

Robertson's mother, Mrs Elsie Robertson of 38 Carrick Knowes Road, said that on one of her visits to Saughton Prison where he was awaiting trial, her son had told her he had left a note in her house. She found the message written on the back of a photograph in the drawer of a dressing-table. It read:

How I will miss you all. To my dear mother. I can't stay and tell you, but immaterial of what I may do or have done I love you with all my heart. Give Willie and Stewarty the same. From your ever loving son, George. PS. I can't stick it any longer. The allegations and hurts I have had all my days from Liz are more than I can stand, as there is not even one item of truth, however, she may suffer by all the ways I am supposed to have treated her.

Mrs Robertson said that her son was usually happy and carefree but, while he was living with his former wife during the fortnight preceding his arrest, he was depressed. She said he was choked with grief over whatever went wrong.

According to the psychiatrist's report, he had examined Robertson three times and found no trace of mental unsoundness or peculiarity of mind. It had not been reported to him that Robertson, while in Saughton Prison, had tried to obtain phenobarbitone tablets to commit suicide, or that he had assaulted a warder who was not connected in any way with his frustration in the attempt to get these drugs.

Robertson had indicated that he realised the very great seriousness of the position in which he was placed and that he might hang. The psychiatrist suggested that, on the night of the murder of his wife and son, and the attempted murder of his daughter, the defendant had suffered an acute brainstorm and was not responsible for his actions.

Crowds awaited admittance to the court for Robertson's trial. He arrived from Saughton Prison in a large dark-blue police car escorted by two police officers. Still wearing a grey gaberdine raincoat, he took his seat in the dock to hear the jury's verdict of 'Guilty as charged' and the judge's death sentence.

Robertson was hanged at Saughton Prison on 23 June 1954, the last murderer to be hanging in Edinburgh before the abolition of the death penalty in 1957 – a sentence reinstated for certain degrees of murder but finally abolished during the '60s.

15 TRON SQUARE, 1973

Map ref. 21

Twenty years later Tron Square witnessed further domestic violence which ended in tragedy. On 16 October 1973 Margaret Bain
murdered her former husband by strangling him with a pair of
tights.

It was the long story of a battered wife. She had married
Andrew Bain in 1941. They were divorced in 1948 but lived
together again later. Mrs Bain told the court that she was not sorry
that he was dead.

In an appalling chronicle of abuse, she told how he was always
aggressive after drinking and had on one occasion burned her
arms with a cigarette and her thighs with a poker. He had tried to
strangle her and had threatened to kill her with a knife. Once he
had fractured her right index finger as well as damaging her
home.

Mrs Bain pleaded guilty and said that on the day of his death
he had been drinking and was sitting in an armchair. An argument had started when she suggested that he should get a job.

At one point he told her that he wanted to die. He then reached
up for a pair of tights which were hanging on a line across the
fireplace and wrapped them around his neck. He invited her to
take hold of an end.

She told the court that Bain kept pulling the tights higher up his
neck. Suddenly she saw that his tongue was going black and his

feet were 'twitching'. She realised that he was not acting and ran to her neighbour's house.

The police were called and found Mrs Bain hysterical. She kept repeating, 'I killed the bastard.'

Later, when cautioned, she had stated, 'After seven years you break up. He kept telling me "tae dae" it – meaning strangle him – so I did.' When asked why she had not attempted to pull the ligature from his neck, she said, 'I still thought he was going to jump up. I thought he was just acting.'

Questioned as to whether she was glad when she saw he was dead, she replied, 'At that moment I was not quite sure what to think. I am not sorry he is dead for what he put me through.'

The professor of forensic medicine at the University of Edinburgh stated that it was conceivable the dead man could have strangled himself. The jury's verdict of 'Not guilty' was unanimous.

27 SOUTH BRIDGE, 1977

Map ref. 22

On the opposite side of the road from Tron – now Hunter – Square is South Bridge where on 26 May 1977 Edward Linton, aged fifty-seven, was found dead in his attic flat at no. 27 shortly after 5 a.m.

A constable on a routine check found the body after climbing to the top of the winding tenement stair. On two previous nights he had seen an electricity board meter card lodged between the door and the jamb. On the third occasion he had knocked on the door and found it open.

The murdered man, a widower, lived alone. There were no other flats in the building occupied by shop premises and the police immediately sealed off the area and began searching for clues, sifting through the piles of rubbish littering the entrance to the stair as they put out an appeal for any witnesses or relatives to come forward.

Linton had been a baker and confectioner with St Cuthbert's Co-operative Association and had retired in August 1976 after twenty-nine years' service. He and his wife had once been well-known exhibition ballroom dancers in the East of Scotland.

In trying to piece together Linton's last hours, the police were faced with an additional problem as it was known that since his wife's death he had become something of a recluse. The post-mortem revealed that he had lain dead for a week before his body was discovered, and could have lain bound but alive for three days before dying of severe multiple injuries, including shattered bones in his fingers, arms and leg and six broken ribs. All the injuries were on the left side of his body, and there were also a number of abrasions on his chest and shoulders and one on his head. His wrists had been bound with flex, and a considerable amount of violence had been used to inflict his horrific injuries. Some were consistent with a weapon such as a hammer, while the abrasions on his lower arms indicated that he had tried to free himself.

On 31 May, five days after the discovery of Linton's body, an anonymous telephone call to the local police led to the arrest of two youths, Alan McCartney aged nineteen and Frank Gallagher aged eighteen, who had broken into the house to get money to go to Wembley.

Gallagher, traced to Craigmillar Castle Terrace, made a statement in which he claimed that McCartney had picked up a hammer and hit the man on the leg. McCartney had also told him to tie Linton's hands and Gallagher had said to the man, 'Your hands, Jimmy', to which the man had replied, 'Certainly, son!' McCartney had then tied the man's mouth with a tie and they left the flat and dumped the hammer. His statement ended with the words 'We were drunk'.

McCartney, living at Fernieside Grove, was an unemployed whisky bond labourer. He said he had met Gallagher drinking in a nearby bar two weeks before going to the flat in South Bridge and Gallagher had asked him if he was going to the England v. Scotland game at Wembley.

'I told him I couldn't because I had no money. He said he knew where to get money but that we'd have to break into a house.'

McCartney claimed that he'd never done a house before but Gallagher kept tormenting him and finally he agreed to go along. The house was a top flat in a stair at South Bridge and stuck in the door was a South of Scotland Electricity Board meter card which indicated that there had been a call to empty the pre-payment meter. Gallagher had said, 'We'll be rich, we'll be rich.'

After kicking the door in, they searched inside and heard footsteps on the stair. They hid behind the front door and, as a man came in, Gallager grabbed him and pushed him into the front door where he fell on the floor.

McCartney said, 'I was going to run out of the house but Gallagher said, "Don't be feart." I took it he knew the man so I stayed.'

Gallagher then put the lights out and McCartney said he heard a thud as somebody fell: 'It was the man and he was greetin'.' When Gallagher put the lights on again he was standing over the man holding a hammer.

McCartney said not to hit him again but Gallagher was laughing and told the man to get his clothes off. He then went through Linton's pockets and bound him, stuffing his mouth with brown paper and gagging him with his own tie. Searching the house, McCartney heard the man moaning and, returning to the room, saw the man lying on the bed with Gallagher hitting him with a hammer. McCartney then 'stuck the heid' on Gallagher, called him 'a dirty bastard' and said he dragged him away and took the hammer from him.

Michael McCartney of Bernard Terrace, twin brother of Alan, said his brother had came to his home and told him he had broken into a house and had been 'raking about'. He had seen Gallagher hitting the man with a hammer and tying flex round him. He said his brother had told him, 'Frank did it!'

Later Michael and Alan were having a drink in a Cockburn Street pub with Gallagher and Michael had asked him what had happened: 'I wanted to know if my brother was telling the truth.' When Gallagher had said it was the truth but that there had been a blanket over the man's head, he had suggested they should go to the flat and see if the man was all right. Gallagher had refused and his brother Alan had said he was not going alone.

Michael said that on another day he and Alan were having a drink at lunchtime. They had left the public house and walked along South Bridge. A police van was parked outside no. 27. Alan bought a newspaper and said, 'The man's dead, the man's dead.'

Michael had to calm him and claimed that his brother had been 'a bag of nerves' ever since. 'He asked me what he should do and I told him, "It's up to you." I didn't want involved.' He also told him 'not to do anything stupid'. Later he heard Alan had been arrested.

Alexander Gallagher said his brother Frank had come home at midnight on 12 or 13 May and said he'd 'screwed a hoose' in the Bridges along with McCartney. 'He told me they had been disturbed by a man and that he had ran out leaving McCartney inside. He didn't know if McCartney had got caught or not.' One of McCartney's fingerprints was found on a wardrobe in the flat.

The verdict of the jury was unanimous. Alan McCartney and Frank Gallagher were both sentenced to life imprisonment.

47 POTTERROW, 1963

Map ref. 23

From South Bridge cross Chambers Street. Across the road is the Old Quad of the University of Edinburgh, once the site of the city's most baffling historic murder.

It was then known as Kirk o'Field, a rural setting on the outskirts of Edinburgh. Bordering the Flodden Wall, it had been an old ecclesiastical settlement and there, in February 1567, Lord Henry Darnley, second husband of Mary Queen of Scots, was lodging in good country air, politely recuperating from 'smallpox' – which was more likely syphilis.

The house was mined and blown up with gunpowder. The intention was that Darnley should go up with it, but he was found in the gardens in his nightshirt. He had been strangled. The Earl of Bothwell and Mary – believed to be lovers – were blamed, but there were other conspirators who desired Darnley's death and the crime has never been satisfactorily explained, a subject for argument and speculation by historians and novelists ever since.*

Move the calendar on 400 years to 12 March 1963, and round the corner in Potterrow an elderly spinster was found by her niece, battered to death in the kitchen of her first-floor tenement flat.

The police were called to the house by Miss Margaret Kempson

---

* *The Dagger in the Crown*, Alanna Knight, Macmillan 2001.

at 5 p.m. They entered through a white-washed pend off Potterrow and found the body of Jane Gorrian, aged sixty-six and a retired cleaner, with extensive head wounds. A sum of money had been stolen and a hunt was started for a man seen three times during the previous week loitering near and in the pend at no. 48 at about 2.15 p.m. each day and again at 3.30 p.m. on the day before Gorrian was killed. He was described by witnesses as aged between fifty and sixty, about 5'10", and wearing a dirty cap – which might be grey – straight on his head and a scarf tied like a muffler round his neck. He had a dirty face and very watery eyes and mouth and carried a dirty handkerchief in his hand which he used to wipe them periodically. He was thought to be wearing brown trousers and white rubber shoes.

There were no lack of witnesses who came forward and John Andrew Geddes, who looked considerably older than his thirty-three years, of 14 Bruntsfield Avenue, was charged with the capital murder of Jane Gorrian, by striking her on the head with a blunt instrument and tying a stocking round her neck. Then he robbed her of a handbag, a deed box, cash, National Savings stamps to the value of £21 5s, a coat, a magnifying glass and a glove.

Geddes denied the charge together with two charges of fraud and one of theft. He also denied pretending to be Thomas Dangerfield Fiddler, a company director, and Maurice Logan, an assistant, as well as denying pretending that he was a police officer who required an oil heater and paraffin oil container for an elderly woman on his beat who was unable to look after herself.

The first fraud charge related to 20 January 1963 in James Gray & Sons, 80 George Street, Edinburgh, when Geddes said he did not have enough money to pay for the articles and wished to make a credit purchase. The second was that Geddes, claiming to be a police officer, induced people to answer questions put to them and to produce documents for him. The theft charge related to the theft of a transistor radio, a watch and £8 from a house in Portobello.

139

At the trial John Geddes, aged sixty-eight, a retired postman, told the court that his adopted son had been a patient in various mental institutions over the years. As a small boy he had had an accident which resulted in temporary blindness and after holding various jobs he had been discharged from the Army. On the day of the murder he had visited his father at Wauchope Road and, as far as his father could see, was his usual self.

Margaret Gorrian Kempson, aged fifty-four, niece of the dead woman, gave her evidence from a wheelchair. She had lived with her aunt since 1937 and, suffering from arthritis, had to go to hospital for regular treatment. Her aunt was a thrifty woman who kept her money inside a deed box inside a locked trunk in her bedroom.

Kempson described two visits to the house by a man who said he was a policeman. After the second visit her aunt became suspicious and, wondering whether he was a real policeman, said she would check up if he came again. She had found her aunt dead and the trunk half-open when she returned from her hospital treatment.

John Andrew Geddes' wife, Phyllis Geddes, aged twenty-seven, also gave evidence. She said they had married in March 1962 and had a daughter, and that he had been an extremely good husband and father. On 12 March he had come in at about 5.45 p.m. and seemed his normal self. A sum of money found in their house by the police had been saved over a period of time by her husband and he had earned a lot as a 'contact man' for some newspaper. This was when he had been an ambulance man and a statement for Income Tax purposes from one newspaper the previous year gave his earnings over the twelve-month period as about £149.

The consultant psychiatrist from Gogarburn Mental Hospital said that in 1953 he had certified Geddes as 'acutely insane'. Recalling the decision, he said he had found Geddes unable to make a plea to the charges of fire-raising in which he had been involved at the time. He also understood that before that date Geddes had been discharged from the Royal Army Medical Corps after attempting suicide.

Admitted to the Criminal Lunatic Department of Perth Prison, he had remained there until 1957. After being transferred to the State Mental Hospital at Carstairs until 1960, he had been sent to Bangour Mental Hospital and had eventually been released on probation.

The psychiatrist reported that, as far as he had been able to ascertain from Carstairs and Bangour, Geddes was a quiet, apprehensive, inoffensive individual, displaying no signs of violence at all. When he examined Geddes in Saughton Prison a few days before the trial he found him 'sane and fit to plead'. But he had the doctrine of diminished responsibility in mind and diagnosed that Geddes had some form of mental abnormality that prevented his recollection of the events of 12 March. Geddes, he felt, could have been suffering from an acute mental disorder in the nature of hysteria or the aftermath of an epileptic seizure.

Guilty was the jury's unanimous verdict and Geddes was sentenced to death on 12 July 1964. His wife appealed to the Queen and four days before he was due to be hanged at Saughton Prison for the capital murder of Jane Gorrian, Geddes was told that he was to be reprieved.

The decision was announced from St Andrews House. The Secretary of State for Scotland, Mr Michael Noble, had advised the Queen to commute the capital sentence to one of life imprisonment.

THE TORSO MURDER

THE TORSO MURDER, 1969

One of Edinburgh's most baffling and horrific murder cases, covering an area stretching from Balerno to Broomhall, was the climax of a ten-year upswing of violent crimes in eastern Scotland, a pattern identical to that in Glasgow and London. This was the so-called 'Torso Murder' when, on 24 March 1969, two female legs were discovered close to road bridges: the first by a railway plate-layer on the Edinburgh–Fife line at Broomhall, west of Edinburgh, and, nine hours later, the second by a woman walking along Bridge Road. She noticed a brown paper parcel lying under two feet of water on the stony bed of the Water of Leith. It emerged that on the previous Saturday a gamekeeper whose home was on the banks of the river had also seen the parcel, but did not realise its significance since rubbish was often thrown there.

The legs were shapely, well cared for and bizarrely covered in good quality nylons. They had been neatly severed from the torso. At first it seemed likely that a vehicle had been used to dispose of the other parts of the body but, considering the adjacent rail track, the police thought it probable that the severed limbs had been thrown from a train. Trains pass frequently on the route to Aberdeen and the North and the discovery point of the first leg was on part of the city's ring route.

The tracks were carefully searched on the Forth–Tay/

Edinburgh–Perth line from Inverkeithing to Kinross. Not since the notorious Ruxton Case in 1935 had Scotland had to deal with such a crime, when Indian-born Dr Buck Ruxton, a GP from Lancashire, had driven up to the Devil's Beef Tub near Moffat to dispose of the dismembered bodies of his wife and maid at the bottom of the ravine.

When the minute search of the railway track yielded a black leather handbag, which was taken in for examination, the Murder Squad realised that the woman was not necessarily from the Edinburgh area. They were anxious to trace anyone who had been behaving suspiciously and to hear of any unaccounted for female members of a family or from neighbours who knew of a missing woman. They wanted information about people not seen for the past few days at home, work or business. They also wanted information about large packages carried by neighbours and vehicles seen in the area where the legs were discovered.

Meanwhile, the hunt went on for the missing torso, arms and head, extending from the foreshore of the Forth from Leith to Cramond and the countryside beyond Balerno towards Lanarkshire. During daylight hours the moorland areas were also extensively searched.

From the legs that had been recovered, the police were able to begin to fit up a description of the missing woman. She was between twenty and forty, and 5' to 5' 2" in height. Anyone who had seen large unattended parcels lying around was advised to report them to the police and it was suggested that children should also be asked regarding any missing members of their family, since excuses for the absence of a close relative were sometimes given to them.

Cinemas screened appeals, the Union Canal was dragged and 20,000 homes were visited. The appeal for missing persons yielded 462 traced throughout Britain and a further 210 accounted for.

And then came the information that the police had grimly

waited for. On 2 May the torso of a woman was found wrapped in blankets in a pine wood on the A73 Biggar to Lanark road, about a mile from the village of Thankerton in Lanarkshire. The discovery was made by a Mr William Townsley, aged thirty-five, who described himself as a scrap metal merchant. Townsley was one of a family of travellers who had been resting for the night in a layby beside the wood. When he left his caravan early on the morning of 2 May, he came across a bundle tied with twine about two-and-a-half feet square lying a short distance from the main road.

He called his uncle and cousin from the caravan. The twine was cut and inside was a woman's torso – without a head or legs. The men got into one of their lorries and drove four miles to Symington Police Station to report the find.

Immediately police from Edinburgh, the Lothians and Lanarkshire converged on the scene. With them were photographic and fingerprint experts.

Leaving their cars they climbed over a fence and walked into the wood, only a mile from the Glasgow–Carlisle road – a forestry plantation and former prisoner-of-war camp site from the Second World War. The layby was sealed off as officers got to work with forensic equipment from the mobile unit, while more than seventy policemen using tracker dogs combed ten acres of woodland in the area.

It emerged that local police had visited the layby at 10 p.m. the previous night after receiving a complaint from a resident about the Townsleys being in the area. A sergeant accompanied by a constable had told the family that they would have to move out by 10 a.m. the following morning. Matthew's father, James Townsley, aged fifty-four, said, 'It is just as well we didn't otherwise the torso might never have been discovered.'

Amongst the list of local missing women was Elizabeth Keenan, whose husband had reported her disappearance two days after the discovery of the severed legs. Her mother, Elizabeth Roberts, lived in Thankerton, at 28 Mill Road, and she confirmed that she had last seen her daughter on 19 March, five days before the legs had been found five miles apart on the outskirts of Edinburgh.

Roberts was very upset by the suggestion that the torso might be that of her daughter Elizabeth, aged twenty-nine, who lived at 40 Wellwood Avenue, Lanark. After a detailed examination, it was found that the severed legs and torso matched. The torso's arms were intact and fingerprints were taken from the hands. The police compared them with those found in the Keenans' house in an attempt to identify the victim.

On Saturday night, 3 May – thirty-eight hours after the discovery of the torso – the head of Mrs Keenan was found by police searching a plantation of young trees on the road known locally as Lang Whang, near Carnwath. James Joseph Keenan, aged thirty-five, a lorry driver's mate, was arrested and charged with his wife's murder.

The massive investigation which led to his arrest and conviction was one of the biggest in the country. At some point every police force in Britain had been involved. But the main credit lies with three local forces, Edinburgh City, Lothians and Peebles (now combined as Lothians and Borders) and Lanarkshire, whose combined efforts solved the Torso Murder and brought James Keenan to justice.

The horrifying facts emerged. After killing his wife with an axe, he had taken her body into the bathroom of his council house at Wellwood Avenue and there, while his fifteen-month-old daughter slept in another room, he had dismembered it, parcelled it up carefully in separate blankets and then cleaned up, washing the axe and hacksaw he had used. The following night he set out in his Vauxhall Victor on an eighty-mile drive which was to take him to Edinburgh. By the time he got home again he had disposed of the body.

For the six weeks after the discovery of the severed legs a team of twenty-six detectives worked fifteen hours a day trying to identify the woman. Pleas to the public were followed by the head of CID appearing on TV to make a further appeal.

Every conceivable line of inquiry was followed up. In the Case of the Missing Torso, in tasks regarded as routine, police detectives were prepared to talk to every one of 10,000 customers of a nationwide store; trace more than 600 missing women in Britain; track down up to 1000 pairs of blankets; link only 113 microscopic fibres with 10,000 pounds of mill floor sweepings; and dip back into British wartime history to identify material in which a young woman's dismembered and headless body was wrapped. And every line of inquiry would have to be followed through to the end if it meant catching a killer.

It was not only a harrowing and particularly grisly case, but for almost six weeks they also had no clue to either victim or killer, with only parts of a young woman's body from which to work. They had little to go on. Six hundred and sixty-eight women were reported missing or unaccounted for in Britain. Tracking them down with police forces throughout the country, 462 of these were eventually traced, and many were not too pleased about that.

Meanwhile, police concentrated on the material wrapping the first leg discovered – a parcel tied with string and knots. Inside the brown paper fashion carrier bag was a piece of dark coloured blanket, and inside that a child's cot sheet. The leg was revealed. But it was the cot sheet that raised new possibilities. About thirty-five miles away in Lanarkshire there was a report of a missing woman – the young wife of James Keenan. And the couple had a fifteen-month-old child. In the case of the second leg, the wrappings included a dishtowel.

The pathologist's report, as well as obtaining the blood-grouping, suggested the dead woman's height was about 5' 2". She was well nourished, about twenty-six or twenty-seven, and the hairs suggested that she was a brunette. The legs had been amputated quite expertly with a saw at mid-thigh. As far as the leg wrappings were concerned, it was noticed that the pieces of blanket

149

found in the two parcels matched, and were believed to be pieces of the same blanket. Inquiries immediately began to trace the origins. Where had it been bought? Who were the manufacturers?

One of the detectives in charge of the investigation, DCI Deland, was intrigued by the brown paper fashion carrier found round the first leg. He noticed that a piece had been torn from it where there had been handwriting. Only one letter remained – it looked like an 'A' but could have also been an 'R'.

Inquiries to paper-bag manufacturers established that this particular one was produced by a firm in Leeds, and their Scottish customers for this type were The Household Supply Co. Ltd, with a head office in Glasgow and twenty branches throughout Scotland. The plan was to visit each of the 10,000 customers of the company's Edinburgh branch and, if need be, to extend the search to thousands more customers of other branches in the Central Scotland area.

Detectives wanted to know about all female members of such households. Were any missing? And they wanted to know to whom such a carrier bag might have been passed on.

DCS William Muncie, head of Lanarkshire CID, was becoming exceedingly suspicious of Keenan's story and demeanour. On one visit to Keenan's home he looked for traces of his wife's footprints so that these could be matched with those of the legs. None were found but Muncie did take away a pair of her shoes and sent these to the scientific branch at Edinburgh. The result was a macabre Cinderella-like shoe-fitting to the legs. The shod feet were X-rayed and the experts agreed that they seemed to fit, but it would be necessary to have some older or more worn shoes just to be sure.

Meanwhile, there was the matter of the blanket. Two pieces, which appeared to comprise one half of an unusual heather-mixture, were shown to Mrs Keenan's mother. Mrs Roberts had initially refused to credit the possibility that the legs might be her daughter's. However, her reaction showed that she did recognise the pieces of blanket.

The discovery of the torso by the Townleys, complete with arms, gave them a lead on fingerprints. The torso also carried a scar consistent with an ovarian operation.

The result was Keenan's arrest on suspicion of murder. When scientific officers scraped together deposits from the U-bend of the bath, basin, toilet and sink, the blood samples were the same type as those of Mrs Keenan. The three pieces of blanket from the legs and torso appeared to make up one blanket, which Mrs Keenan's mother reluctantly recognised as one of three she had given to replace some that had been burnt. A grey blanket that had been round the torso was also shown to her and she produced its neighbour. A multi-coloured tea towel and the cot sheet from one of the legs were identified by her as similar to items which should have been in Keenan's house but were no longer there.

When Keenan was charged with the murder of his wife, he was asked to empty his pockets. From the hip pocket he produced a piece of string, adhering to which was a weft of material similar to the blanket from the legs and torso. The forensic laboratory took the string and matched twelve fibres of different colours and compositions with fibres from the murder blanket. Also among the yarn and string from Keenan's pocket was a twist of blue cellulose acetate fibre which matched a similar twist of fibre from the blanket on one of the legs.

The investigation stretched out to the woollen mills of England, where scientific officers learned that yarn of this type was made from a blend of fibre sweepings from mill floors and pulled rag waste material. Considering that each blend, which would be in the region of 5000–10,000 1b in weight, was gathered from a wide variety of sources, then the yarn fibre – and especially the colour content – would be peculiar to the number of blankets which each blend produced – estimated at between 500 and 1000 pairs.

The lack of nylon or any of the other synthetic polymer fibres in the yarn from the pocket or from the blanket suggested that the yarn had been spun prior to 1941, as synthetic fibres were not in common use prior to this date. Bearing this out was the fact that the blanket bore a wartime utility label.

Finally, it transpired that the blankets had been a present to Mrs Keenan's mother from a cousin who had bought them at a sale over twenty years before.

Keenan was taken from Barlinnie Prison and on Friday, 9 May was driven the twenty-five miles to Lanark. His head covered by a blanket, and wearing a black jacket, white shirt without a tie, grey flannels and brown shoes, he was handcuffed and almost hidden between the officers for the fifty yards between the police station and the courthouse.

The background of the case was related to family matters between Keenan and his wife. After a marriage of ten years, they were anxious to have a child and had a baby daughter, Veronica Jane, born in January 1968. They were devoted to the child.

On his third appearance in court Keenan, smartly dressed in a midnight-blue suit, white shirt and matching blue tie, pleaded guilty to the murder of his wife and admitted that he had assaulted her and struck her repeatedly on the head with an axe or other instrument. The court were told that Mrs Keenan was last seen by a relative on Wednesday, 19 March. One of a family of six, Betty Keenan was a country girl. She was devoted to her widowed mother, Mrs Roberts, and at weekends Keenan used to drive her to her mother's at Mill Road – in the same car he later used to dispose of his wife's body.

On the day of the murder, his brother-in-law called and an arrangement was made whereby Keenan was to take his wife's sister to Law Hospital. On the next day he drove his sister-in-law to the hospital and made mention of his wife having left the house. Afterwards he called at his mother-in-law's house and said his wife had 'walked out on him' the previous night.

Keenan went to Lanark Police Station on 26 March and reported that his wife had left him. This was two days after the discovery of the severed legs and the police had many reports of missing women. However, a detailed examination of the two legs produced a description of the victim which was consistent with it being Mrs Keenan but no positive identification was obtained.

Keenan was seen again by the police on 15 April and made a statement regarding his wife's departure, but not until the torso was found on 2 May was Keenan interviewed later that day at Lanark and put in a cell. On the following morning, before he was due to appear in court, he confessed to the murder.

He was extremely contrite and said he wanted to tell what he did to his wife and why he did it. He said she was threatening to go away and take the baby with her.

'She kept repeating she should never have had the baby and that I would never see the baby again. I must have just lifted this axe and hit her. The next thing I remember she was on a chair and had a tie around about her neck. I realised what I had done and must have panicked.

'I drank a bottle of whisky and remember being violently sick in the bathroom. My wife was lying in the bath cut up. I remember that I had a hacksaw in my hand and that I was sick. I wrapped up the legs, the torso and the head in a blanket and paper and I must have fallen asleep.

'I wakened up in the morning and took the parcels with the pieces of body down to my car. I then took the baby over to my mother and drove my wife's sister to hospital.

'I then went to her mother's – this was later on that day – and to her aunt's and told them my wife had gone and left me.

'Then that night I got rid of the parcels. I drove in the car and threw one parcel out at one bridge and another at another bridge. I got out of the car and threw them over the bridges. I then threw one in a wood on the Lang Whang and the other I carried into a wood on Thankerton Moor.'

On the way back from court Keenan said he wanted to show where he had put the head and directed the police to the place where it had been found.

153

Keenan was born and brought up in Lanark, one of a family of eleven children. He had trained as an apprentice jockey in his early twenties and became a well-known punter at Lanark and Hamilton race courses. He worked for a time at Douglas Water Pit near Lanark and then with a coal merchant in Thankerton.

Very conscious of his small stature, he started weight training at a local club to help increase his strength – an activity that earned him the nickname 'Tarzan'. Keen on playing dominoes, he was also a regular drinker at the Gordon Hotel.

Employed at Ross Motors, a pump attendant spoke of Keenan's apparent unconcern during the murder investigation. 'He just didn't seem to care. A week after his wife went missing he came in here at night and I asked him about it. He said his wife felt he thought more of their baby than he did of her and that was why she had left.'

Keenan was sent to prison for life – the final chapter of the most unusual and bizarre murder case in Scotland in the twentieth century.

INDEX

Killers (italics); victims (v)

INDEX